A NIGHT
OF ROYAL
CONSEQUENCES

A NIGHT
OF ROYAL
CONSEQUENCES

SUSAN STEPHENS

MILLS & BOON

First published in Great Britain 2017
by Mills & Boon, an imprint of HarperCollins*Publishers*
1 London Bridge Street, London, SE1 9GF

Large Print edition 2018

© 2017 Susan Stephens

ISBN: 978-0-263-07357-7

MIX
Paper from
responsible sources
FSC™ C007454

This book is produced from independently certified
FSC™ paper to ensure responsible forest management.
For more information visit www.harpercollins.co.uk/green.

Printed and bound in Great Britain
by CPI Group (UK) Ltd, Croydon, CR0 4YY

For my most excellent editor, Megan,
who is a joy to work with.

CHAPTER ONE

As FUNERALS WENT, this was as grand as it got. As tradition demanded Luca, who was now the ruling Prince, arrived last, to take his place of honour in the packed cathedral. He was seated in front of the altar beneath a cupola with images painted by Michelangelo. Towering bronze doors to one side were so stunningly crafted they were known as the 'gateway to paradise'. Tense with grief, Luca was aware of nothing but concern that he'd pulled out all the stops for a man to whom he owed everything. Flags were flown at half-mast across the principality of Fabrizio. Loyal subjects lined the streets. Flowers had been imported from France. The musicians were from Rome. A procession of priceless horse-drawn carriages drew dignitaries from across the world to the cathedral. Luca's black stallion, Force, drew his father's flag-draped coffin on a gun carriage with the Prince's empty boots reversed in the stirrups. It was a poignant sight, but the proud horse held his head high, as if he knew his precious cargo was a great man on his final journey.

As the new ruler of the small, but fabulously wealthy principality of Fabrizio, Luca, the man the scandal sheets still liked to call 'the boy from the gutters of Rome', was shown the greatest respect. He'd moved a long way from those gutters. Innate business acumen had made him a billionaire, while the man he was burying today had made him a prince. This magnificent setting was a long way from the graffiti-daubed alleyways of Luca's childhood where the stench of rotting rubbish would easily eclipse the perfume of flowers and incense surrounding him today. The peeling plaster and flyposting of those narrow alleyways replaced by exquisite gothic architecture, the finest sculpture, and stained glass. In his wildest dreams, he had never imagined becoming a prince. As a boy, it had been enough to have scraps he stole from bins to fill his belly and rags to cover his back.

He inclined his head graciously as yet another European princess in need of a husband acknowledged him with an enticing smile. Fortunately, he'd retained the street smarts that warned him of advantage-takers. He wouldn't be chaining himself down to a simpering aristo any time soon. Though he could do nothing about the testosterone running through his veins, Luca conceded wryly. Even freshly shaved and wearing dress uniform, he looked like a swarthy brawler from the docks. His appearance had been one thing his adoptive father, the late Prince, had been unable to refine.

Well over six feet tall and deeply tanned, with a honed, warrior's frame, Luca couldn't be sure of his parentage. His mother had been a Roman working girl. His father, he guessed, was the man who used to pester her for money. The late Prince was the only parent he remembered clearly. He owed the Prince his education. He owed him everything.

They'd met in the unlikely setting of the Coliseum, where the Prince had been on an official visit, and Luca had been stealing from the bins.

He had not expected to come to the notice of such a grand man, but the Prince had been shrewd and had missed nothing. The next day he had sent an *aide de camp* with an offer for Luca to try living at the palace with the Prince's son, Max. They would be company for each other, the Prince had insisted, and Luca would be free to go if he didn't like his life there.

Young and street smart, Luca had had the sense to be wary, but he'd been hungry, and filling his belly had been worth taking a chance. That chance had led to this, which was why honouring the Prince was so important to him. He held his adoptive father in the highest esteem, for teaching him everything about building a life, rather than falling victim to it. But the Prince had left one final warning on his deathbed. 'Max is weak. You will follow me onto the throne as my heir. You must marry and preserve my legacy to the country I believe we both love.'

Clasping his father's frail hand in his, Luca had given his word. If he could have willed his strength into a man he loved unreservedly, he would have done that too. He would have done anything to save the life of the man who'd saved him.

As if reading Luca's thoughts, his adoptive brother Maximus glared at him now from across the aisle. There was no love lost between the two men. Their father had failed to form any sort of relationship with Max, and Luca had failed too. Max preferred womanising and gambling to statecraft. He'd never shown any interest in family at all. He favoured the hangers-on who flocked around him, lavishing praise on Max in hope of his favour. Luca had soon learned that, while the Prince was his greatest supporter, Max would always be his greatest enemy.

Picking up the order of service to distract himself from Max's baleful glare, Luca scanned his father's long list of accomplishments and titles with great sadness. There would never be such a man again, a thought that made him doubly determined to fulfil his pledge to the letter. 'You are a born leader,' his father had told him, 'and so I name you my heir.' No wonder Max hated him.

Luca hadn't looked for the honour of being heir to the throne of Fabrizio. He didn't need the money. He could run the country out of pocket change. Success had come when he'd nagged his father to let him bring Fabrizio up to date, and had insisted on studying tech at university. He'd gone on to become one of the most successful men in the industry. His global holdings were so vast his company almost ran itself. This was just as well as he had to turn his thoughts to ruling a country, and to filling the empty space beside him.

'If you fail to do this within two years,' his father had said on his deathbed, 'our constitution states that the throne will pass by default to your brother.' They both knew what that meant. Max would ruin Fabrizio. 'This is your destiny, Luca,' his father had added. 'You cannot refuse the request of a dying man.'

Luca had no intention of doing so, but the thought of marrying a simpering princess held no appeal. The royal marriage mart, as he thought of it, didn't come close to his love of being with his people. He would leave here and travel to his lemon groves in southern Italy, where he worked alongside the other holiday workers. There was no better way for him to learn what concerns they had, and to do something to help. The thought of being shackled to a fragile china doll appalled him. He wanted a real woman with grit and fire inside her belly.

'There are good women out there, Luca,' his father, the Prince, had insisted. 'It's up to you to find one. Pick someone strong. Search for the unusual. Step off the well-trodden path.'

At the time Luca had thought this wouldn't be easy. Looking around today, he thought it impossible.

As funerals went, this one was small, but respectable. Callie had made sure of it. It was small in as much as the only people to mourn her father's passing, other than herself, were their next-door neighbours, the rumbustious Browns. It was a respectable and quiet affair, because Callie had always felt she should counterbalance her father's crude and reckless life. There couldn't be two of them wondering where their next meal was coming from. If it hadn't been for her friends, the Browns, laughing with her at whatever life threw up, and reminding her to have fun while she could without offending other people, as her father so often had, she'd have been tearing her hair out by now.

The Brown tribe was on its best behaviour today—if she didn't count their five dogs piling out of their camper van to career around the country cemetery barking wildly, but they'd given Callie a glimpse of what a happy family life could be, and, in her heart of hearts, love and a happy family was what she aspired to.

'Goodbye, Dad,' she whispered, regretting everything they'd never been to each other as she tossed a handful of moist, cool soil on top of the coffin.

'Don't worry, love,' Ma said, putting her capable arm around Callie's shoulders. 'The worst part is over. Your life is about to begin. It's a book of blank pages. You can write anything on it. Close your eyes and think where you'd like to be. That's what always makes me happy. Isn't it, our Rosie?'

Rosie Brown, Callie's best friend and the Browns' oldest child, came to link arms with

Callie on her other side. 'That's right, Ma. The world's your oyster, Callie. You can do anything you want. And sometimes,' Rosie added, 'you have to listen to the advice of people you trust, and let them help you.'

'Anywhere ten pounds will take me?' Callie suggested, finding a grin.

Rosie sighed. 'Anywhere has to be better than staying round the docks—sorry, Ma, I know you love it here, but you know what I'm getting at. Callie needs a change.'

By the time they'd all crammed into the van, Callie was feeling better. Being with the Browns was like taking a big dose of optimism, and, after the lifetime of verbal and physical abuse she'd endured keeping house for her father, she was ready for it. She was free. For the first time in her life she was free. There was only one question now: how was she going to use that freedom?

'Don't even think about work,' Ma Brown advised as she swivelled around in the front seat to speak to Callie. 'Our Rosie can take over your shift at the pub for now.'

'Willingly,' Rosie agreed, giving Callie's arm a squeeze. 'What you need is a holiday.'

'It would have to be a working holiday,' Callie said thoughtfully. 'I don't have enough money to go away.' Her father had left nothing. The house they'd lived in was rented. He'd been both a violent drunk and a gambler. Callie's job as a cleaner at the pub just about paid enough to put food on the table, and then only if she didn't leave the money lying around for him to spend at the bookies.

'Think about what *you'd* like to do,' Ma Brown insisted. 'It's your turn now, our Callie.'

She liked studying. She wanted to better herself. She aspired to do more than clean up the pub. Her dream was to work in the open, with fresh air to breathe, and the sun on her face.

'You never know,' Ma added, shuffling around in her seat again. 'When we clear out the house tomorrow your father might have left a wad of winnings in his clothes by mistake.'

Callie smiled wryly. She knew they'd be lucky to find a few coppers. Her father never had any money. They wouldn't have survived at all without the Browns' bounty. Pa Brown had an allotment where he grew most of their vegetables himself, and he always gave some to Callie.

'Don't forget you can stay with us as long as you need to, until you get yourself sorted out,' Ma Brown called out from the passenger seat.

'Thank you, Ma.' Leaning forward, Callie gave Ma's cheek a fond kiss. 'I don't know what I'd do without you.'

'You'd do more than all right,' Ma Brown insisted firmly. 'You've always been capable, and now you're free to fly as high as your mother always intended. She used to dream about her baby and what that baby would do. It's a tragic shame that she didn't live to see you grow up.'

She'd soon find out what she could and couldn't do, Callie thought as the Browns and their dogs piled out of the steamed-up van. She couldn't stick around for long. She'd be a burden to the Browns. They had enough to do keeping their own heads above water. Once her father's debts were paid, she'd go exploring. Maybe Blackpool. The air was bracing there. Blackpool was a traditional northern English seaside town with bags of personality, and plenty of boarding houses looking for cleaning staff. She'd research jobs there the first spare minute she got.

It would have been a grim task sorting through her father's things the next morning, if it hadn't been for the cheerful Browns. Ma checked every room, while Callie and Rosie sorted everything into piles for the charity shops, things that could possibly be sold, and those that were definitely going to the dump. The sale pile was disappointingly small. 'I never realised how much rubbish we had before,' Callie admitted.

'Mean old bugger,' Ma Brown commented. 'He probably took it with him,' she added with a sniff.

'I doubt there was anything to find in the first place,' Callie placated. She knew her father's ways only too well when it came to money.

'Nothing left after he'd been gambling and boozing, I expect,' Ma Brown agreed, disapprovingly pursing her lips.

'Well, that's where you're both wrong,' Rosie exclaimed with triumph as she flourished a five-pound note. 'Look what I've found!'

'Well, our Callie!' Ma Brown began to laugh as Rosie handed it over to her friend. 'Riches indeed. What are you going to do with it?'

'Nothing sensible, I hope,' Rosie insisted as Callie stared at the grubby banknote in amazement. 'It's not even enough to buy a drink, let alone a decent meal.'

She would rather have her father back either way, Callie thought, which was strange after all the years of trying to win his love, and coming to accept that there was no love in him. 'I'll put it in the charity tin at the corner shop,' she mused out loud.

'You'll do no such thing,' Ma Brown insisted. 'I'm taking charge of this,' she said as she snatched the banknote out of Callie's hand.

'Think of it as an early Christmas present from your father,' Rosie soothed when she saw Callie's distress. 'Ma will do something sensible with it.'

'It would be the first gift he'd ever given her,' Ma Brown grumbled. 'And as for doing something sensible with it?' She winked. 'I've got other ideas.'

'Sounds good to me,' Callie said with a weak smile, hoping the subject would go away now.

Knowing her friend was upset beneath her humour, Rosie quickly changed the subject and it wasn't spoken of again. The next Callie heard of their surprise find was at supper with the Browns. When the girls had finished clearing up, Ma Brown folded her arms and beamed, a sure sign of an announcement.

'Now then, our Callie, before you say anything, we know you don't gamble and we know *why* you don't gamble, but just this once you're going to take something from me, and say thank you and nothing else.'

Callie tensed when she saw the five-pound scratch card Ma Brown was holding out.

'You'll need something to scratch the card,' Pa observed matter-of-factly as he dug in his pocket for some loose change.

'Close your eyes and imagine where all that money's going to take you,' Rosie urged, glancing at the other Browns to will them to persuade Callie that this could be a good thing if she got lucky.

'All *what* money?' Callie had to smile when the Browns fell silent. Silence was such a rare occurrence in this household, she couldn't let them down.

'It's time for a change of luck,' Rosie pressed. 'What have you got to lose?'

The Browns had been nothing but kind. The money she'd get from the scratch card would likely take her as far as the hearth to toss it in the fire when it proved a dud. 'Close my eyes and imagine myself somewhere I've always dreamed of…'

'Open your eyes and scratch the bloody card,' Ma Brown insisted.

As everyone burst out laughing Callie sat down at the table and started scratching the surface of the card.

'Well?' Ma Brown prompted. 'Don't tease us. Tell us what you've got.'

'Five. Thousand. Pounds.'

No one said a word. Seconds ticked by. 'What did you say?' Rosie prompted.

'I've won five thousand pounds.'

The Browns exploded with excitement, and the

next few hours were spent in a fury of mad ideas. Opening a pie and peas shop next to the pub, a sandwich bar to serve the local business park. 'I want to give my money to you,' Callie insisted.

'Not a chance.' Ma Brown crossed her capable arms across her capacious chest, and that was the end of it.

Callie made up her mind to put some of it aside for them, anyway.

'You could buy all the rescue dogs in the world,' one young Brown called Tom said optimistically.

'Or a second-hand car,' another boy exclaimed.

'Why don't you spend it all on clothes?' one of the girls proposed. 'You'll never get another chance to fill your wardrobe.'

What wardrobe? Callie thought. Her worldly possessions were contained in a zip-up bag, but she smiled and went along with this idea and they all had some fun with it for a while.

'It isn't a fortune and our Callie should do something that makes her happy,' Pa Brown said. 'It should be something she's always dreamed of, that she will remember for ever. She's had little enough fun in her life up to now, and this is her chance.'

The room went quiet. No one had heard Pa Brown give such a long speech before. Ma Brown always spoke for him, if the dogs and his brood weren't drowning him out.

'Well, our Callie,' Ma Brown prompted. 'Have you got any thoughts on the subject?'

'Yes, I do,' Callie said, surprising herself as she thought of it.

'Not Blackpool,' Rosie said, rolling her eyes. 'We can go there any weekend we like.'

'Well?' the Browns chorused, craning forward.

Reaching for the television guide, Callie opened it out flat on the table. There was a double-page spread, a travel feature, showing vibrant green lemon groves hung heavily with yellow fruit. A young family of husband, wife and two children capered across the grass, staring out towards unimaginable adventures. The headline read: *Visit Italy.*

'Why not?' Callie said as all the Browns fell silent. 'I can dream, can't I?'

'You can more than dream now,' Ma Brown pointed out with her usual common sense.

But by this time, Callie was already putting her dream on the back burner in favour of a far more realistic plan. Perhaps a weekend in a small coastal resort nearby. She could look for a job while she was there.

'Think big. Think Italy,' Rosie insisted.

'That would be a proper memory, all right,' Pa Brown agreed.

Callie stared out of the window at a grey, dismal scene. Like the rented house where she'd grown up, the Browns' opened out onto the street, but the people passing by outside had their shoulders hunched against the cold. The photo in the magazine promised something very different. Rather than traffic fumes and bed socks, there'd be sunshine and fruit trees. She glanced at the page again. It was like a window opening onto another world. The colours were extraordinary. The people in the shot might be models, but they surely couldn't fake that happiness, or the sense of freedom on their faces.

'Italy,' Ma Brown commented, her lips pressing

down as she thought about it. 'You'll need some new clothes for that. Don't look so worried, our Callie. You won't need to spend much. You can do very well on the high street.'

Rosie clearly had other ideas and frowned at her mother. 'This is Callie's chance to have something special,' she whispered.

'And she should,' Pa Brown agreed, picking up on this. 'Goodness knows, she's gone without long enough.'

'A mix, then,' Ma Brown conceded. 'High Street with designer flourishes.' And with that healing remark the family was content.

'Amalfi,' Callie breathed as copying the idea in the magazine took shape in her mind. The thought of a short trip to Italy made her head reel with excitement. A change of scene was what she needed before she started the next phase of her life, and the win had made it possible.

'All that wonderful sunshine and delicious food, not to mention the music,' Rosie commented with her hand on her heart as she thought about it.

All that romance and the Italian men, Callie's inner devil whispered seductively. She blanked out the voice. She had always been cautious when it came to romance. She'd had too many duties at home to be frivolous, and too many opportunities to witness first-hand how violent men could be.

'Come on, our Callie. Where's your sense of adventure?' Ma Brown demanded as all the Browns murmured encouragement.

She was free to do as she liked, so why not don a glamorous dress and designer heels for once? A few days of being not Callie was more than tempting, it was a possibility now. Just this once, the good girl could unleash her fun side—if she could still find it.

CHAPTER TWO

HE NOTICED THE woman sitting at the bar right away. Even from behind she was attractive. It was something in the way she held herself, and her relaxed manner with his friend, Marco, the barman. He'd just ended a call with Max, and was in the worst of moods. Max had lost no time in Luca's absence causing unrest in Fabrizio. Max had been a thorn in his side since they were boys. Thanks to his mischief, Luca should not be visiting his beautiful lemon groves on the Amalfi coast, but should return immediately to Fabrizio, but this was an annual pilgrimage to a place he loved amidst people he cared for, and nothing, not even Max, could distract him from that. Though on this occasion, he could only spare a couple of nights here.

The woman was a distraction. She was watching everyone come in through the mirrors behind the bar. Was she waiting for a lover? He felt a stab of jealousy and wondered why he cared when she could just as easily be waiting for a family member, or for a friend.

He'd dropped by the hotel to invite Marco to the annual celebrations at the start of the lemon-picking season. He and Marco had grown up together, as Marco's father had worked for the late Prince. Standing at the end of the bar where he could talk discreetly to Marco when he was free, he saw the woman clearly for the first time. She was confident and perky, and obviously enjoying the chance to trial the Italian language. Laughter lit her face when she got something wrong and Marco corrected her.

Feeling mildly irritated by their obvious rapport, he returned to working her out. Her profile was exquisite, though she seemed unaware of this, just as she seemed unaware of the appeal of her slight, though voluptuous body. She was understated, unlike his usual, sophisticated type. He couldn't help but be intrigued. Dressed impeccably, though plainly for this setting in one of the coast's most famous hotels, as if she was playing a role, she was almost too perfect. Her red hair was lush and shiny, cut short for practicality, rather than fashion, he guessed. Her eyes were green and up-tilted, giving her a faintly exotic look. A light tan and freckles suggested she'd been here no more than a week and lived somewhere cooler.

This was a lot of thought to expend on a woman who seemed unaware of his interest. Or was she? His groin tightened when she turned to stare at him boldly and was in no hurry to look away.

Interesting.

'Good evening.' After politely acknowledging the woman, he gave Marco a look that left his friend in no doubt that Luca wished to remain incognito.

Sensing mischief afoot, Marco grinned. They exchanged the usual complicated handshake, while the woman looked on with interest. She was even more beautiful than he'd first thought. Her scent was intoxicating. Wildflowers. How appropriate, he thought as Marco left them to go and serve another customer. 'Can I buy you a drink?'

She levelled a stare on his face. 'Do I know you?'

The bluntness of her question took him by surprise, as did her forthright tone. Out of the corner of his eye, he saw Marco lift a brow. His friend would call security if Luca gave the word, and the woman would be politely moved on. An almost imperceptible shake of Luca's head knocked that idea out of court.

'My name is Luca,' he told her as he extended his hand in greeting.

She ignored his hand. Intelligent eyes, framed by long black eyelashes, viewed him with suspicion.

'I don't believe we've met,' he pressed, waiting for her to volunteer her name. 'I don't bite,' he added when she continued to withhold her hand.

'But you're very persistent,' she said, making it clear there would be no physical contact between them.

Persistent? Outwardly, he remained deadpan.

Inwardly, he cracked up. Women referred to his charm and thought him attentive. Clearly, this woman had other ideas. 'What would you like to drink?'

'Fizzy water, please,' she replied.

Turning to Marco, he murmured, *'Aqua frizzante per la signorina, e lo stesso per me, per favore.'*

'Sì, signor,' Marco replied, serving up two sparkling waters.

Her gaze remained steady on his as she took her first sip. There wasn't a hint of simpering or recognition in her eyes, just that desirable mouth smiling faintly. Even now she'd had time to think about it, he was a man in a bar and that was it. She had no idea who he was, and would trust him as far as a glass of water was concerned, but no further. If she was unaware that his face had been plastered all over the news lately, since he'd ascended the throne of Fabrizio, something big must have happened in her life.

So, beautiful mystery woman, he mused as she returned his interest coolly, who are you, and what are you doing in Amalfi?

* * *

Straightening the short silk skirt on her designer dress, Callie wished she had worn the Capri pants Rosie had insisted were essential to Callie's Italian adventure instead. So chic, Rosie had said as Callie had turned full circle, wishing she could get away with a new pair of jeans and a top. The Capris were still in the wardrobe upstairs in the hotel, as she'd been unsure which shoes to wear with them.

At least Capris would have been decent. The dress was anything but. Far too short, it was enticing. She could only imagine what this incredible-looking man had thought when he'd first seen her perched at the bar. How could she convey the fact that she wasn't here for *that* type of business, and that this was, in fact, a holiday? The thought of an Italian adventure had excited her, but she hadn't envisaged such a dynamite opening scene. She fell well short compared to the other, more sophisticated women in the bar. There was barely enough fabric in her skirt to cover her fundamentals. She couldn't move for fear of it riding up, and with her naked thigh so close to the man's denim-clad muscles, that was a pressing concern.

'You didn't tell me your name.'

She turned to look at him as the dark velvet voice, with its seductive hint of an Italian accent, rolled over her. Strange how sound could send shivers spinning up and down her spine. Her chin felt as if it had half a universe to travel, as she moved from scrutinising his muscular thighs, to staring into a pair of mesmerising black eyes. Mesmerising and amused, she noticed now. He hadn't missed her fascination with the area below his belt. Her cheeks burned as she volunteered with a direct stare into his eyes, 'My name is Callista.'

His lips pressed down in the most attractive way, drawing her attention to the fact that his mouth was almost as expressive and beautiful as his eyes. 'Greek for most beautiful,' he remarked. 'That explains everything.'

'Really?' She did her best to simper and then hardened her tone. 'I've heard of people being born with silver spoons in their mouths, but yours must have been coated in sugar.'

He laughed, and then affected a wounded expression. 'I'm crushed,' he exclaimed, holding both hands to his powerful chest.

'No, you're not,' she insisted good-humouredly, starting to like him more now he'd proved to have a sense of humour. 'You're the most together person I've ever met.'

He smiled. 'So what is Callista the huntress doing on her own in a hotel bar?'

'Not what you think,' she flashed back.

'What I think?' he queried.

'What are you doing on your own in the bar?' she countered.

He laughed again, a blinding flash of strong white teeth against his impressive tan. 'I'm here to see the barman. What's your excuse?'

'A holiday.' She levelled a stare on his face. 'What do you do for a living?'

The bluntness of her question seemed to take him by surprise, but he soon recovered. 'This and that.'

'This and that, what?' she pressed.

'I guess you could call me a representative.'

'What do you sell?'

'I promote a country's interests, its culture, industry and people.'

'Ah, so you're in the tourism business,' she exclaimed. 'That's nice.' And when he nodded, she asked, 'Which country do you represent?'

'Are you staying here long?' he asked, changing the subject.

The fact he'd ignored her question didn't escape her notice and she gave him a suspicious look. Then, obviously deciding it couldn't do any harm to tell him a little more, she added, 'Not long enough.'

She was enjoying the man's company and decided to prolong the exchange. He excited her. It was no use pretending when every nerve ending she possessed was responding with enthusiasm to the wicked expression in his laughing black eyes. She'd never flirted before, and was surprised to find she rather liked it. This man could turn her insides warm and needy with a look.

'Have you been dancing yet?' he enquired, shooting her an interested look.

'Is that an invitation?'

'Do you want it to be?'

'No, sadly.' She gave him a crooked smile. 'These shoes are killing me.' Twirling a foot, she stared ruefully at the delicate designer shoes with their stratospheric spiky heels. *Could anyone walk in them?*

'You could always slip them off and dance,' he suggested.

As he spoke a band struck up for the evening's entertainment somewhere outside on the terrace. Imagine dancing beneath a canopy of stars, she thought. How romantic. She glanced at her companion, and immediately wished she hadn't. He really did have the wickedest black eyes, which, for some reason, made her think of slowly stripping off her clothes while he watched. She shivered inwardly at the thought. What she should be doing was making it clear that she didn't pick up men in bars. She should collect up her things, get down from the stool and walk away. It was that easy.

Sex with him would be fun. And seriously good.

What was wrong with her? This wasn't the type of simmering heat she'd read about in novels and magazines, but hot, feral lust, that promised very adult pleasures indeed.

'You are extremely entertaining, *signorina*.'

'Really?' Goodness, she hadn't meant to be. He certainly was. Sensuality emanated from him. If she embarked on her Italian adventure with Luca, it could only lead to one place. *Fantastic!* Callie's inner harlot rejoiced, so now the thought of lying close to him, skin to skin, with those strong, lean hands controlling her pleasure—

'Signorina?'

'Yes?' She blinked and refocused on his eyes... his disturbingly experienced eyes. However attractive and compelling she found him, she had to be careful not to take these newfound flirting skills too far. *So the adventure of a lifetime is over before it begins?* The adventure of a lifetime was great in theory, but in practice it threatened all sorts of unknown *pleasures*—dangers, Callie corrected her inner demon firmly. She had more sense than to let things go too far. Concentrating fiercely on her glass of water, she tried not to notice Luca's brutal masculinity as it warred with her inner prude. She gave up in the end.

He'd won this point. He was far better at flirting than she was.

What else was he good at?

Stop that now! Didn't she have enough to contend with—a crotch-skimming skirt, and heels custom-made to prevent a stylish exit—without going head to head with a sex god in jeans?

'Another *aqua frizzante, signorina*?'

How did Luca make that simple question sound so risqué? 'Yes, please.'

Oh, so her sensible self was on holiday too?

She wanted to know more about him. What was wrong with that? Chances like this didn't come around every day. *So shoot me if I'm easy.* She wasn't ready to leave yet. And, anyway, why should she be the one to go?

Marco quickly refilled her glass and Luca handed it to her. She sucked in a sharp breath as their fingers touched. He was like an incendiary device to her senses. Using the mirror behind the bar, she surveyed the other men in the room to see if any compared. No, was the simple answer. They were all without exception safe-looking guys, dressed neatly in business suits. There was no one else slouched on one hip, wearing extremely well-packed jeans and a crisp white shirt open a few buttons at the neck to reveal a shading of dark hair. She jumped guiltily when she realised that Luca was staring back at her through the mirror.

'Taking everything in?' he suggested with that same wicked look.

He couldn't be interested in her. It didn't make any sense with so many attractive women in the bar. Had he heard she'd won some money? He might be a particularly good-looking con man on the make, though he didn't seem in need of cash and Marco the barman seemed to know him. Having survived her father, she had no intention of falling for a good-looking man simply because he was charming.

Falling for him?

'You're frowning, *signorina*,' Luca murmured in a way that made all the tiny hairs on the back of her neck stand to attention. 'I hope I'm not the cause of your concern?'

'Not at all,' she said briskly as his direct stare sped straight to her core where it caused havoc all over again. On any level Luca was concerning. Lacking airs and graces, with his rugged good looks he could easily be a roustabout from the docks. Equally he could be a practised seducer. And now was not the time for her body to shout hallelujah! Instead, she should be thanking him for the drink and walking away. 'Would you like a nut?' she asked instead. Luca grinned and raised a brow in a way that thrilled her. 'Before I eat them all,' she added in a tone that told him not to tease as she pushed the bowl towards him.

'It would be easier and far tastier to come out to supper with me,' he said, angling his chin to stare her in the eyes.

Not a chance. That would be courting danger.

'Supper?' Luca pressed. 'Or more nuts?'

She glanced with embarrassment at the almost empty dish—and gasped with shock when Luca took hold of her hand. She had never felt such a shock at a physical connection with another human being. The disappointment when she realised he'd only taken hold of her hand to steady it as he poured the last few nuts from the dish onto her palm was humiliating.

'Enjoy your supper, *signorina*,' he said, straightening up.

'You're going?'

'Will you miss me?'

'Only if I run out of nuts.'

He huffed a laugh that made her heart race like
crazy. 'You could come with me.'

She could singe her wings and crash back down
to earth too. 'No, thank you.' She smiled, a little
wistfully, maybe, but she knew she was doing the
right thing. Luca was like a magnet drawing her
into danger with those dark laughing eyes. She
was enjoying this newfound flirting skill far too
much. 'Don't let me keep you from your supper.'

'I choose to be here.'

The way he spoke made breath hitch in her
throat. The way he looked at her made everything
inside her go crazy. It was everything about him,
the Italian accent, his deep, husky voice, and his
ridiculous good looks, and perhaps most of all the
mesmerising stillness of his magnificent body.
She was hypnotised—and determinedly shook
herself round.

'*Signorina?*'

He was waiting for her decision.

'Enjoy your supper.' She wanted to go with him. She wanted to be a bad girl for once in her life. Bad girls had more fun. But then she would have to live with regret. How could she not? She would regret sleeping with him and not knowing him better. She would regret not sleeping with him, and never having the chance again.

'Enjoy your nuts—'

She couldn't believe it when he walked away. Oh, well, that was that, then. Everything went flat when he walked out of the door, and he didn't look back. He hadn't suggested they meet again, and he hadn't asked for her number. She'd probably done herself a favour, Callie reassured herself. He'd expect too much, more than she was prepared to give, anyway.

Saying goodnight to Marco, she got down from the barstool. She felt impatient with herself as she walked away. She couldn't miss a man she didn't know. She'd feel better once she was back in her room. She might have dressed up tonight, as per Rosie and Ma Brown's instructions, but she was still Callie from the docks inside. But not for long, Callie decided when she reached her room. She couldn't hang around the hotel aimlessly; she had to *do* something—get out, see more of the real Italy. This trip was supposed to be an adventure. She wasn't tied to the past, or frightened of the future. Roll on tomorrow, she thought as she climbed into bed, and whatever it might hold.

As soon as he got back to the *palazzo* he called Marco. 'Who is that woman?'

'Signorina Callista Smith? Staying at the hotel on her own, if that's what you're asking, my friend.'

'Am I so obvious?'

Marco barked a laugh down the phone. 'Yes.'

'Do you know anything else about her?'

'Only that she comes from the north of England and that her father died recently, so this is a rebooting exercise for Callie. That's how she described it while we were chatting. And that's all I know about her.'

'Okay. It explains a lot, though I'd guessed some of it.'

'And?' Marco prompted.

'And it's none of your business,' Luca told his old friend. 'See you on the estate for the celebrations tomorrow night?'

'The start of the lemon-picking season,' Marco confirmed. 'I wouldn't miss it for the world, but can you spare the time? I thought Max was kicking off in Fabrizio.'

'I have controls in place to keep Max on a leash.'

'Financial controls?' Marco guessed.

'Correct,' Luca said calmly. Max's allowance was generous under their father's rule, and was even more so now that Luca had the means to increase it. Max had never liked to work and with no other source of income he looked to Luca to support him.

'And before you ask,' Marco added, 'Signorina Smith is booked into the hotel for another few days.'

'You've been checking up on her?'

Marco laughed. 'You sound suspicious. Do you care?'

He was surprised to discover that he did. 'Back off, Marco.'

'That sounds like a warning.'

'And maybe I've discovered a conscience,' Luca suggested. 'She's innocent and she's alone, and you are neither of those things.'

'You feel responsible for her already?' Marco commented knowingly. 'This sounds serious.'

'I'm a caring citizen,' Luca remarked dryly.

'I'll do as you say,' Marco offered with his customary good humour. 'And I'll watch with interest to see how long your concern for Signorina Smith's innocence lasts.'

He told Marco what he could do with his interest in Callista Smith in no uncertain terms, reminded him about the celebrations, and then cut the line.

What was he doing? He was a driven man with a country to care for, and a practically out-of-control brother to deal with. And he had to find a bride to provide an heir and continue the dynasty. He shouldn't be wasting time on contemplating an affair—wouldn't be, if he hadn't found Signorina Smith so appealing. He had to remind himself that she was an ingénue with her life ahead of her, and, yes, everything to learn. If they never saw each other again it would be better for both of them. She should learn about sex and the harsh realities of life from a man who could make time for her.

Just don't let me run into that man, Luca reflected dryly as he sank into the custom-moulded seat of his favoured bright red sports car. He'd have to kill him. *No!* He had no time to waste on romancing a woman who might have intrigued him tonight, but who would surely bore him by tomorrow when she proved to be as shallow as the rest.

Gunning the engine, he drove into town with his head full of Callista Smith. He planned to eat at his favourite restaurant. She should have been with him. Top international chefs worked at the *palazzo*, but Signorina Smith had put him in the mood for more robust fare. Tomorrow he would work alongside his seasonal staff in the lemon groves. In lieu of more challenging distractions, for which he had to thank Signorina Smith for providing some very entertaining images to keep him awake tonight, he'd fuel up on good food instead.

'Hey, Luca... Alone tonight?' The restaurant owner, who'd known Luca since he was a suspicious child tagging along behind his newly adoptive father, rushed out of the kitchen to give him a warm hug.

'Unfortunately yes. But don't worry. I can eat enough for two.'

'You always had a huge appetite,' the elderly owner approved.

True, Luca mused dryly as he ran his experienced eye over the women seated at the tables. They all stared at him with invitation in their eyes, but not one of them had the power to hold his interest. Not like Callista Smith.

She was surely the most ungrateful person in the world, Callie concluded as she woke to yet another day of sublime Italian sunshine. And frowned. She was staying in the most beautiful place imaginable in the most fabulous hotel, and yet still she felt as if something was missing. But how could that be, when she was nestled up in crisp white sheets, scented with lavender and sunshine, wearing the ice-blue, pure cotton nightdress trimmed with snowy white lace that Ma Brown had said Callie must have for her trip of a lifetime.

If money can't make me happy, what can I do next?

Well, she'd spent most of the money on staying at this hotel, so she wouldn't have to worry about her win on the scratch card and what it felt like to have some extra cash at her disposal for too much longer, Callie concluded with her usual optimism. Leaping out of bed, she threw the windows open and the view snatched the breath from her lungs. Steep white cliffs dropped down to pewter beaches where the shoreline was fringed by the brightest blue water she'd ever seen. Closing her eyes, she inhaled deeply. Flowers and freshly baked bread, overlaid by the faint tang of ozone, prompted her to take a second breath, just so she could appreciate the first.

What was so terrible about this?

She was lonely, Callie concluded. She missed the Browns. She missed her colleagues at work. Maybe it hadn't been much fun at home with her father being drunk most of the time, but the

Browns more than made up for it, and even caring for her father had taken on a regular and predictable pattern. She still felt sad when she thought about him and his wasted life. He could have made so much more of himself with his natural charm and undeniable good looks, but instead had chosen to gamble and drink his life away, putting his trust in unreliable friends, rather than in his daughter Callie, or the Browns.

It was no use dwelling on it. She was determined to make a go of the rest of her life, which meant that decisions had to be made. She wasn't going to sit around in the hotel doing nothing for the rest of her stay. Nor was she going to monopolise Marco and risk bumping into the man with the devastating smile again. Luca was out of her league, the stuff of fairy tales. She had wracked her brains to try to find a film star or a celebrity who could eclipse him and had come up short. There was no one. It wasn't just that Luca was better looking, or had presence to spare, but the fact that he was so down to earth and made her laugh. And thrill. She liked him so much it frightened her, because that wasn't normal, surely? You couldn't just meet a man in a bar and never stop thinking about him…imagining his arms around her, his lips pressed to hers…body pressed to hers… That was ridiculous! She was being ridiculous, Callie concluded, pulling away from the window to retreat into the airy room. She could fantasise about Luca all she liked—well, had done for most of the night, but she had enough sense to stay well away.

'Room service…'

She turned and hurried across the room to answer the door. 'Sorry I took so long. I slept in today.'

'I can come back,' the young maid offered.

'No. Please,' Callie exclaimed. 'Your English is very good. Can I ask you something before you go?'

'Of course. My name is Maria,' the young woman supplied in answer to Callie's enquiring look. 'If I can help you, I will.'

Maria wasn't much older than Callie. Her long dark hair was neatly drawn back, but her black eyes were mischievous, and she had the warmth of Italy about her that Callie was fast becoming used to. 'If you wanted to work outside in the sunshine, Maria—we don't get very much where I come from,' Callie explained ruefully. 'Where would you look for a job?'

'Oh, that's easy.' Maria's face brightened. 'This is the start of the lemon-picking season when the demand for casual labour is at its highest. There's a big estate belonging to the Prince just outside town. They're always looking for temporary staff at this time of year.'

'The Prince's estate?' Callie exclaimed. 'That sounds grand.'

'It's very friendly,' Maria assured her. 'It must be for the same people to come back year after year.'

'Do you think I could get a job there?'

'Why not?' Maria frowned. 'But why would you want to work as a picker?'

Callie could see that it must seem odd for her to be staying at a five-star hotel, yet jumping at the chance to work in the fields. 'I need a change,' she admitted, 'and I'd love to work in the open air.'

'I can understand that,' Maria agreed. 'I'd go today if I were you, so you don't miss the party.'

'The party?' Callie queried.

'There's always a party at the beginning of the season,' Maria explained, 'as well as at the end. Apart from exporting lemons around the world, they make the famous liquor Limoncello on the Prince's estate, and his parties are always the best.'

'Is the Prince very old?'

Maria snorted a laugh. 'Old? He's the hottest man around.'

Two of the best-looking men in one town seemed impossible, but as she wasn't likely to bump into the Prince, and was determined to avoid Luca, her heart could slow down and take a rest. 'I can't thank you enough for this information,' she told Maria.

'If there's anything else you need, anything at all, Signorina—'

'Call me Callie. You never know when we'll meet again,' Callie added, thrilled at the prospect of having a real goal to aim for.

'In the lemon groves, maybe,' Maria suggested.

'In the lemon groves,' Callie agreed, feeling excited already at the thought of working in lemon groves that she'd only seen in a photograph before.

She was excited and couldn't wait to embark on her new plan, Callie mused as she took her shower. She wouldn't be Callie from the docks for much longer, she'd be Callie from the lemon groves, and that had a much better ring to it.

This was his favourite place in the world, Luca concluded as he swung a stack of crates onto the back of a truck. Hard, physical labour beneath a blazing sun, surrounded by people he loved, who couldn't have cared less if he were a prince or a pauper. Max had been dealt with for now, and was cooling off after his drunken rampage in the local jail, Luca's royal council had informed him. He should take this last chance to celebrate at the party tonight, his most trusted aide Michel had insisted. 'I'll come back right away, if you need me,' he'd told Michel. Luca had never resented the shackles of royal duty. He felt humbled by them, and honoured that the late Prince had trusted him with the responsibility of caring for a country and its people. The only downside was picking a princess to sit at his side, when so far none of the candidates had appealed to him.

To lie at his side, to lie beneath him, to give him children.

He ground his jaw and thought about Callista. She could lie at his side and lie beneath him, though he doubted she'd remain calm or accepting for long. If he were any judge, she'd want to ride him as vigorously as he thought about riding her, with pleasurable thoroughness and for the longest possible time. Callista had more spirit in her little finger than all the available princesses put together possessed in their limp and unappealing bodies. But the fact remained: he had to choose a wife soon. His father's elderly retainer, Michel, had point-blank refused to retire until Luca took a wife. 'I promised your father I'd watch over you,' Michel had said. 'What this country needs is a young family to inject life and vitality into Fabrizio, to lead the country forward into the future.'

He'd sort it, Luca concluded. He always did. The buzz of interest surrounding him at his father's funeral suggested suitable breeding stock wouldn't be too hard to find. A very agreeable image of Callista chose that moment to flash into his mind. Callista naked. Giving as good as she got, verbally, as well as in every other way. She might be young and inexperienced, but her down-to-earth manner promised the type of robust pleasure that an insipid princess would be incapable of providing.

And how does this advance my hunt for a wife?

Loading the last crate of lemons, he groaned as he remembered Michel's words: 'Yours will be a bountiful reign with a harvest of children as abundant as the lemons on your estate,' Michel had assured him. Right now it was Luca's face that looked as if he'd sucked a lemon when he contemplated the current selection of brides.

Work over, he tucked his hands into the back pockets of his jeans and eased his shoulders, grimacing as he thought about the stack of neglected folders on his desk. Leafing through them had confirmed his worst fears. All the princesses were excellent contenders for the role of his wife, but not one of them excited him.

What would Callista be doing now? *She'd bet-*

ter not be sitting at that bar. He'd drag her out, and—

Really? He grinned, imagining her reaction to that. There was nothing insipid about Callista. She wouldn't fall into line, or be content to bask mindlessly in luxury while working dutifully on creating an heir and a spare. Even Michel would find Callista difficult to lure into the royal fold.

Grazie a Dio! The last thing he needed was a headstrong woman fighting him every step of the way!

But a bolt of pure lust crashed through him as he imagined her in his arms. Finding a suitable princess could wait a few days.

Callie stared up in wonder at the royal gates marking the boundary of the Prince's estate. They were everything she'd expected and more. They were regal and imposing with gilt-tipped spears crowning their impressive height, while lions, teeth bared, grinned down at her. 'Hello,' she murmured, giving them a wink. The lions scowled back.

'Very welcoming,' she managed on a dry throat.

Should she be using another entrance? Was there a back entrance? Well, it was too late now. She was here. And then she spotted a notice. It was only about twelve feet high. 'Numbskull,' she muttered. Turning in the direction indicated by the bright red arrow, she walked over to a disappointingly modern control box attached to the far side of the gate. Pressing the button, she jumped with surprise when a metallic voice barked, *'Sollevare la testa, si prega.'*

'I'm sorry, but I don't speak Italian very well...'

'Look up, please,' the same metallic voice instructed.

She stared at the sky.

'At the camera.'

Okay, numbskull squared, that small round lens just in front of me is a camera!

The metallic voice hadn't shown any emotion, but Callie could imagine the person behind it rolling their eyes. Finally, she did as instructed.

'The photograph is for security reasons,' the metallic voice grated out. 'If you don't wish to enter the estate, please step back now.'

'No—I do. I mean, yes. I'm here to apply for a

job. I'm sorry if I should have used another entrance…' Her mouth slammed shut as the massive gates swung open.

'Report to the foreman in the first barn you come to.'

'Yes, *signor*…um…*signora*?' The sex of The Voice would remain a mystery for ever, Callie thought as she stepped into a very different world.

This was a world of control and order, Callie concluded, as well as extreme magnificence on every level. Awestruck, she stared down the length of an incredible avenue composed of a carpet of glistening, white marble beads. At the end of this lay a pink stone edifice, bleached almost white by the midday sun. Both elegant and enormous, the *palazzo* boasted turrets and towers that could have come straight from a book of fairy tales. Cinderella's castle, she mused wryly. The driveway leading up to the palace was broad and long, with stately cypress trees lining the route like sentries. Butterflies darted amongst the colourful flowerbeds lining her way, and birds trilled a welcome as she walked along, but there was no sign of the barn The Voice had referred to.

'*Hey! Per di qua!* This way!'

She turned at the sound of friendly voices to see more pickers following her into the palace grounds. They'd halted at what she could now see was the shrubbery-concealed entrance to a pathway.

Callie scolded herself as she hurried to join them. There was another sign, and it was a huge one, but she'd missed it completely, being too busy ogling her surroundings. The sign read, *'Benvenuto ai nostro personale stagionale!'* Even she knew what that meant. 'Welcome to our temporary staff!'

It was certainly a warmer greeting than the stained sheet of lined paper pinned up on the noticeboard outside the pub, which warned staff to use the back door not the front, on pain of immediate dismissal.

The pickers had waited for her and were all in high spirits. She blended right in with denim shorts and a loose cotton top, teamed with a pair of market-find trainers. She was ready and excited for whatever lay ahead. This was an adventure. This was what she'd been waiting for. This was something to tell the Browns.

It was good news to hear she could start right away and be paid in cash if she wanted. That suited Callie. She planned to check out of the posh hotel and move to a small bed and breakfast in town to extend her stay. She'd already called to confirm the B & B had rooms. She wanted to get to know the real Italy, and, with her father's example behind her, she knew better than to fritter her money away. She'd tasted the high life, and was glad to have done so, but had come away feeling slightly let down. This was so much better, she concluded as she trooped out of the barn with the other pickers. There were no airs and graces here, and, more significantly, no need to wear those excruciatingly painful high-heeled shoes.

The Prince's estate was like a small town. She hadn't guessed how big it was from the road. There were dozens of gangs of pickers working throughout the spectacular lemon groves. This was heaven, Callie thought as she straightened up and paused for breath. Yes, the work was hard, but the sun was warm, the scent of lemons was intoxicating. She had thick gloves to protect her hands and a tool to pick the lemons that were out of reach. The camaraderie was incredible. Everyone wanted to help the newcomers. The party Maria had told her about at the hotel was definitely on tonight, and all the pickers were invited. What could possibly be better than this?

She soon returned to the rhythm of picking. With a lightweight bucket tied around her waist, dropping fruit into it as she went, she loaded the lemon gold into crates that were taken away on gleaming tractors. By the time the blazing sun had mellowed into the amber glow of early evening, she felt as if she'd been working there all her life.

She'd even made a new friend called Anita, a big, bonnie woman, as Ma Brown would have called her, with a ready smile as big as Texas. Anita came from the north of England each year to pick lemons, to feel the sun on her face, to prepare her for the long, cold winter, Anita said. 'I'm on my own,' she'd explained to Callie, 'but when I come here, I have a ready-made family.'

That was when Callie told Anita about the Browns. 'It's people that make things special, isn't it?' she'd asked.

This wasn't just a great way to extend her stay in Italy, Callie concluded as Anita offered to show her the way to the cookhouse, this was an entirely new slant on life, if she had the courage to seize it.

Seize it she would, Callie determined. Her limbs might be aching from all the unaccustomed exercise, but she felt exhilarated for the first time in years. This, *this* was freedom.

CHAPTER THREE

HER ADVENTURE HAD only just begun, Callie realised as excitement for the upcoming party built inside her. Anita had shown her to one of the many well-groomed courtyards surrounding the palace where the celebration was to be held. She couldn't help glancing through the brilliantly lit windows of the palace, to see if she could spot the Prince. Of course, there was no one who looked remotely like a prince, and there was no special buzz in the crowd, so he probably wasn't here. Anita and she accepted a small glass of iced Limoncello from a passing waiter and started to chat. They hadn't been talking long before Callie felt compelled to turn around. She gasped. 'Luca?'

'Someone you know?' Anita asked with surprise.

'Sort of,' Callie admitted. She'd just caught a

glimpse of him, but now there was a crowd clustering round, so she could only see the top of his head. She wasn't surprised by all the interest. It was his magnetism that had first gripped her. 'He didn't tell me he worked here,' she told Anita.

'He's a regular—are you all right?' Anita had been about to say something else about Luca, but was responding to the look on Callie's face.

'I'm absolutely fine,' Callie insisted on a dry mouth. Which was an absolute lie. She had to put her glass down and cross her arms over her chest to hide her arousal as Luca looked at her. And he didn't just glance her way. Their stares locked and held.

'Uh-oh. He's coming over,' Anita warned. 'I predict things are about to change for you,' Anita commented sagely. She had to nudge Callie, who was as good as in a trance. 'Better make myself scarce…'

'No, Anita! Stay—' Too late. Anita had already disappeared into the crowd.

Luca saluted Callie with a bottle of beer, and his slanting smile of recognition was infectious and made her smile too. Her heart raced out of control. It was so exciting to see him again. *Too exciting.* She should follow Anita. What was she thinking of, standing here, waiting for a man who looked as if he ate brass tacks for breakfast with a virgin on the side?

Quite simple, Callie concluded, lifting her chin. She didn't run away from anything, and she wasn't about to start now.

And he was quite a magnet. Luca looked better than ever in his banged-up work clothes. Swarthy-faced, with an unruly mop of thick black hair and an indecent amount of sharp black stubble, he was everything better avoided for those in search of a quiet life. *But I'm here in search of adventure*, Callie reminded herself with a secret inner grin. Tousled and rugged, with scratches on his powerful forearms and hard-muscled calves, he even looked sexy when he wiped smudges of dirt from his face with the back of his arm. The bonfire behind him was throwing off flames that provided the perfect showcase for a man who looked like a dark angel from hell come to wreak havoc on novice flirters.

'Luca,' she said pleasantly as he came over, acting as if her senses weren't reeling.

'Signorina Callista Smith,' he countered with a slanting grin. 'What a pleasant surprise.'

'You know my name?' He must have been talking to Marco the barman, Callie realised. She wasn't sure how she felt about being discussed by the two men.

'You can't expect to be ignored, signorina.'

As Luca made a mock bow, she tried not to notice they'd become the centre of attention. She didn't flatter herself that he'd picked her out for any particular reason. If he was a regular as Anita had suggested, she was fresh meat.

His top was tight and skimmed the waistband of his low-slung shorts. It was impossible not to notice the arrow of dark hair that swooped beneath his zipper, or indeed the quite preposterous bulge that lay beneath. To say he looked amazing was an understatement. Even when she tried to focus on something harmless, like his tanned feet in simple thonged sandals, she realised they were sexy too. Her interest travelled up his legs to powerful calves, and on again to where she definitely shouldn't be looking. She had to stop this right now, and *concentrate*!

No! Not there!

She was about to meet a very challenging man for the second time, and she'd better be ready for it, Callie warned herself firmly. Fixing her gaze on Luca's darkly amused face, she determined not to let her gaze wander, but then thought, why not stare? Luca had never been shy about staring at her, and interest wasn't a one-way street. His bronzed and muscular torso, barely covered by the ripped and faded top, invited attention. He was an outstanding specimen. A statue should be raised in the town square for everyone to admire.

'Nice to see you at the party,' he said, smiling in that faint way he had that made her body burn. 'I hope they're serving nuts tonight.'

She gave him a look, half smile, half scolding. He'd stopped within touching distance. His heat enveloped her. And that voice. Dark chocolate tones strummed her senses until they were clamouring for the sort of pleasure she guessed Luca knew only too much about. He towered over her in a way that blocked out the light, which was enough to warn her to be careful. She didn't stand in anyone's shadow. 'Are you here on your own?' she asked, diplomatically stepping away.

'I am,' he confirmed.

His voice curled around her, making her skin tingle. 'No one waiting for you back home?' she enquired casually.

'My dogs, my cats and the horses,' he said.

'I think you know what I mean,' she insisted.

'Do I?' Luca stared at her in a way that made heat curl low in her belly. 'Do you always put people you've only just met through the third degree?'

When they look like you, and have who knows what secrets, yes, I do, she thought. 'That depends who I'm talking to,' she said.

'So why do I get the third degree?'

'Do we have enough time?' she demanded, and when he laughed, she said honestly, 'I just didn't expect to see you here, so it's a bit of a surprise.'

'A surprise I hope you're getting used to?'

His black eyes were dancing with laughter, so, responding in kind, she shook her head and heaved a theatrical sigh. 'I'm trying to be tactful, and I realise now that blunt is much easier for me.'

'I'm with you there,' he said. 'So be blunt.'

'Are you married?' she asked flat out. 'Or do you have a partner, a special friend?'

Luca grinned. 'You weren't joking about blunt.'

'Correct,' Callie confirmed. 'Before I say another word, I need to know where I stand.'

'Do I look married?'

'That's not an answer to my question,' she complained. 'In fact, I'd call it an evasion.'

'I'm not married,' Luca confirmed as she turned to go. She stilled when he caught hold of her arm. His touch was like an incendiary device to her senses. 'I'm unattached, other than being briefly joined to you,' he said as he lifted his hand away. She felt the loss of it immediately. 'Does that satisfy your moral code?'

'My moral compass is pointing in a more hopeful direction,' she agreed.

'You're an intriguing woman, Callista Smith.'

'Callie.' She enjoyed the verbal sparring with him. 'And you must have led a sheltered life.'

He laughed out loud at that suggestion, making her wish they could carry on provoking each other for the rest of the night. Electricity sparked between them. He made her feel good. Primal attraction, she thought. Sex, she warned herself flatly. Who couldn't think about sex with Luca?

He looked like a natural-born hunter who thought he'd found his prey. While under her blunt manner, Callie was sugar and spice and all things nice, and determined to remain that way. Her body could argue all it liked that sugar and spice could still enjoy verbal sparring, but she had no intention of taking things any further. Luca might be everything she'd fantasised about while she was on her knees scrubbing floors in the pub, but this was reality, not a dream world, and the safest thing she could do now was leave. 'I was about to go home,' she explained, glancing away down the drive.

'Aren't you enjoying yourself?'

Too much. 'I am.' She couldn't lie. She'd enjoyed everything about today, and now the food smelled amazing, the band was playing, and it was a beautifully warm evening beneath a canopy of stars. And then there was Luca. 'But I've got work tomorrow.'

'So do I,' he said smoothly.

'You're making this difficult for me.' And hard to breathe, she silently added.

'Why deny yourself the reward for a hard day's work?'

That depended on the reward. Good grief, he was beautiful! His stillness reminded her of a big, soft-pawed predator preparing to pounce. She didn't need a wake-up call, Callie concluded. She needed a bucket of ice-cold water tossing over her head.

'Hey, Luca!'

They both swung around to see Marco coming over. It broke the tension for a while as Luca greeted Marco, but once the two men were done with complicated handshakes and Marco moved on, the two of them were alone again. 'I thought you'd have gone in search of nuts by now,' Luca remarked dryly.

'I was waiting to say goodbye to you.'

'Ah.'

Was he convinced, Callie wondered, or had he guessed that she was trapped like a rabbit in headlights by his brazen masculinity?

'So why are you here, mystery woman? You're staying at a five-star hotel, but work in the fields picking lemons?'

'What's wrong with that?' she challenged.

'Nothing.'

'Well, now we've got that sorted out, I'll say goodnight.' To give him his due, there was no more questions. Luca shrugged and stood aside to let her go, but as she passed he reached out to smooth a lock of hair from her face. His touch thrilled her. Her skin tingled, and her nipples tightened, while tiny pulses of sensation beat low down in her belly.

'Stay,' he insisted. 'You'll have more fun.'

That was what she was afraid of. 'Should I be flattered by your suggestion?' she asked coolly, searching his eyes.

'No,' he said bluntly. 'You should be on your guard.'

She made a point of glancing around. 'Are there many predatory men at this party?'

'None that stand a chance of getting close to you.'

'Will you keep them away? I would have thought you had better things to do.'

'And I thought you were leaving,' he countered.

'I am.'

He could hardly believe it when she walked away. This wasn't a woman he could tease into his bed, but a woman to be reckoned with. Good. He needed a challenge. There was only one woman who could hold his interest tonight. He could hardly believe the transformation from butterfly at the bar, to working girl in the lemon groves. It was a good mix. That stubborn chin clinched it for him. He was done with insipid. She had a great walk too. He feasted his eyes as she walked away from him with her head held high and her shapely butt swaying provocatively beneath the simple clothes. She hadn't a clue who he was. He doubted it would have made any difference. Status meant nothing to Callie, as proved by her easy transition from luxury living in the five-star hotel, to some of the hardest physical work in the area.

The sun had been kind to her today. Flushed from physical activity, she looked good enough to eat, something he'd put on hold until later in the evening, he reflected dryly. He watched as she met up with her friends. She was more relaxed than she'd been at the hotel. Laughing easily, she mimed words when the different languages spoken became a problem. Nothing seemed to faze her. Apart from him.

She was comfortable around everyone, as he was, and far more beautiful than he remembered. Young and natural—even the smear of dirt on her neck only made him think about licking it off. It was time he stopped thinking about Callie naked in his arms, or he'd be walking around the party uncomfortably aroused.

And, before he committed himself to taking her to bed, there were questions to be answered. Why was she picking fruit for a few euros a day when she was staying at a five-star hotel? Was it just for the experience? Who was funding her?

Why was she in Italy? Was this a holiday or an escape? If she was escaping, from what? He had no intention of allowing Max to lure him into a honey trap that could discredit Luca, and expose the principality of Fabrizio to corruption beneath his half-brother's rule. It was time to find out more.

As he approached Callie her friends melted away. 'Where are they going?' she asked with surprise.

They were diplomatically giving him space. Callie couldn't help but be oblivious to the dynamics that existed between a prince and his people. However much he would have liked it to be different, obstacles between him and Utopia were not in his gift to remove.

'Anyone would think you'd got the plague,' she said, bringing a comic slant to bear on the situation.

'Let's hope it's not that serious,' he said, loving the way she could pop the pomposity bubble before it even had chance to form. She had raw, physical appeal, he mused as she stared up at him. It was all too easy to imagine her limbs

wrapped around him as she sobbed with pleasure in his arms. 'Dance?' he suggested, curb-
ing baser needs.

'Not if I can help it,' she exclaimed.

The response was pure Callie. 'Why not?' he
demanded, play-acting wounded.

'Because I have two left feet and the sense of
rhythm of a hamster on a wheel.'

He shrugged. 'Should be interesting. I'm a fast
mover myself.'

She raised a disapproving brow, but her eyes
betrayed her interest.

'Perhaps I can slow you down?' he suggested.
'Show you an alternative to racing to the finish?'

Her cheeks flushed red. She'd got the sexual
message in his words loud and clear, but she hit
him with a blunt response. 'You must be wearing steel-capped boots to feel so confident. And
I'm going to sit this one out.'

He was nowhere near finished and caught hold
of her arm. Momentum thrust her against him.
She felt sensational, strong, lithe, and yet softly
plump in all the right places. She was so tiny compared to him, but they fitted together perfectly.

'You're taking a lot for granted.' She frowned, but made no attempt to move away.

'I don't see you rushing off,' he countered softly.

'Caveman.'

'Nut freak.'

'Nut freak?' She stared into his eyes. Her lips were just a tempting distance away.

'You're quaint,' he said, meeting her jade-green eyes head-on.

'Quaint?' she queried.

'Old-fashioned.'

She appeared to consider this, and then said, 'There's nothing wrong with tradition. Someone has to take responsibility for keeping standards high.'

Yes. That was him. He stared at a mouth he could have feasted on until she fell asleep with exhaustion. 'Talk to me,' he murmured.

'About what?' she asked, her brow crinkling in enquiry.

He didn't care. He just loved to watch her lips move as she goaded him. The thought of teasing those lips apart with his tongue to claim all the dark recesses of her mouth, along with every-thing else, fired him up until the hunger to take her was all-consuming. 'That dance we talked about?'

'You talked about.' But she didn't resist when he steered her towards a space that miraculously, as far as Callie was concerned, had opened for them on the packed dance floor.

When Luca pressed her close she gasped at the intensity of feeling. She was conscious that peo-ple were staring at them and whispering, which she guessed was only to be expected when she was dancing with the hottest man at the party. Why he'd chosen her to dance with, she had no idea. She hadn't exactly made it easy for him. When he nuzzled her hair aside and kissed her neck, she didn't care what his reasons were. She didn't care about anything. The world and every-one in it simply dropped away.

CHAPTER FOUR

RISK VERSUS PLEASURE, Callie thought as she flicked a glance into Luca's eyes. Even the briefest look sent heat surging through her. She could trust herself for one dance, she decided, which might have had something to do with the fact that when Luca took hold of her hand a thrill raced through her. When his other hand slipped into the hollow in the small of her back, she could think of nothing but closer contact. Fighting the urge, she kept a sensible distance between them. Other couples had made space for them, so there was no need to cling to him like a limpet.

Luca was really popular, she realised as they started to move to the music. They were attracting lots of interested glances and smiles. In fact, she would call it more of a buzz, so maybe the Prince was close by. She glanced around and realised that she wouldn't know the Prince if she tripped over him. Everyone was probably wondering how she got so lucky, but she couldn't shake the feeling that she was missing something. There was no chance to dwell on it. It was far more important to keep her wits about her. Dancing with Luca was a high-risk sport, she concluded as the sinuous melody bound them closer together. There was only thing more intimate they could do and be this close, and that was to make love—

She could put that out of her head right now! She was going to have one dance, and then she was going home. To pull away from Luca before the music ended would be rude. To fall into the trap of relaxing in his arms was stupid. Control would be her watchword. *At least for now.* Another, far more reckless side of Callie wanted to know why she couldn't see this adventure out. She wasn't Callie who scrubbed floors for a living now, but Callie from the lemon groves, who had a whole world of adventure tucked up inside her.

She made herself relax. Luca was right about

dancing with him being easy. For some reason her feet seemed to know what to do. Her body moved instinctively with his. They could have been alone on the dance floor. She looked up to see him smiling a lazy, confident smile. He was good. He was very good. Luca might look rugged and tough, but when it came to seduction, he was smooth. So long as she was aware of it, she'd be okay, Callie reassured herself as they danced on.

But he must feel her trembling with arousal. Her body was on fire for him. Her heart was banging in her chest. She'd never played such dangerous games before. Luca was so brazenly virile she couldn't think straight. She wanted to lace her fingers through his hair, and explore his body. She wanted to feel his sharp black stubble rasp her skin, and his firm, curving mouth tease hers into submission. *While his big strong hands position me for pleasure...*

No! She had to leave now.

But she didn't.

And then an annoying drone buzzed overhead. 'It's only just checking who's around,' Luca reassured her when she looked up.

'Like we're so important,' she said dryly. 'I guess the Prince must be around.'

'It's a natural precaution when there's a crowd,' Luca explained.

Hmm. She loved to watch his mouth tilt at the corners when he smiled. 'You've worked here before, so you're used to it,' she pointed out, 'but this is all new to me.' *And how!* And how fabulous, Callie thought as the music started up again, and one dance segued smoothly into two.

'Tell me about home for you,' Luca prompted.

'I'm from a small town in the north of England.'

'What's it like?'

His hands were looped lightly around her waist as he pulled his head back to stare at her. A sensible question was welcome. A return to reality was exactly what she needed when their bodies were an electric hair's breadth apart. But how to explain to a man who lived in one of the most beautiful countries in the world that her life back home was not like this? She settled for the truth. 'I'm very lucky. I have the best of neighbours, a good job, and wonderful friends.'

'So you live alone?' he pressed as they danced on.

It was hard to concentrate on anything while she was this close to Luca, but she shook her mind back to the facts. 'I lived with my father until recently. He died a short time before I came to Italy.'

'I'm very sorry.'

'He was killed in a drunken brawl,' she explained. Luca had sounded genuinely concerned, and she didn't want to mislead him, but her eyes brimmed as she said this. It had been such a tragic waste of life. 'The world keeps turning,' she said, to deflect Luca's interest from the confusion on her face. Guilt had always played such a large part in her thinking where her father was concerned. She had never had any influence over him, but had always wished she could have changed things for the better for him.

'And now you're spreading your wings,' Luca guessed, bringing her back on track.

'I'm trying different things,' she confirmed, brightening as she thought about the short time she'd been in Italy. 'I love it here. I love the warmth of the people, and the sunshine, the glamour of a party beneath the stars—who wouldn't love being here on the Prince's estate? I feel free for the first time in a long time,' she admitted carelessly. 'Sorry. My mouth runs away with me sometimes.'

'No. Go on,' Luca encouraged. 'I'm interested. I want to hear more.'

She was careful not to add the word adventure to her gush of information. He would definitely get the wrong idea. She told him a little more, and then his arms closed around her. His embrace was worryingly addictive and people were packed around them on the dance floor, making dancing close inevitable. Luca was easy to talk to and soon she was telling him things that perhaps she shouldn't, like the camaraderie down the pub where she worked that could so easily erupt into violence when people had had too much to drink.

'*Dio*, Callie, how could your father let you work there?'

She frowned. 'No one gave me permission, and it was a well-paid job. Good, honest work,' she emphasised, and then she laughed. 'They had to pay their staff well, in order to keep them in such a rough area.'

'It sounds horrendous,' Luca remarked, not seeing anything amusing in what she'd said.

'We needed the money,' she said honestly, 'and there aren't too many options where I come from.'

Luca was a passionate Italian male, Callie reminded herself, and they could be very protective. He might look hard as rock, but he was no brute. And she was no saint, Callie thought as his hard thigh eased between hers. She tried using force of will to pretend nothing was happening, but that was the biggest fail yet. He was so big and she was so small that relaxing against him soon became snuggling into him, which felt ridiculously good, almost as if it was supposed to be. Music quickly restored her moral compass when the beat speeded up. She thought he'd let her go, lead her off the dance floor, but instead he caught her closer still.

'You're a good dancer.'

'Only because you lift me off my feet.' She laughed, then reviewed what was happening to her body while they were brushing, rubbing, nudging. It was both sensational and addictive. She wanted more. She wanted to toss her moral compass away.

As if sensing the way her thoughts were turning, Luca whispered in her ear, 'I'm sure you've had enough dancing for now.'

She pulled back her head to stare into his eyes, which was dangerous, because now she discovered she was addicted to danger too. The camera drone chose that moment to intrude. 'If the person behind those controls wants to take a better look at us, why don't they just come down here and say so?'

'I doubt we're the sole object of the controller's attention.'

'You could have fooled me.' She glared at the drone. 'Do you think it's so interested because the Prince is here?'

'Possibly,' Luca agreed.

'I haven't seen him yet. Have you? I mean, you've worked on the estate before, so you must know him.'

'I'm offended,' Luca said, half grinning, which

suggested he wasn't offended at all. 'All you want to talk about is the Prince.'

'It's something to tell them about back home.'

'What about me?' he growled.

'Don't look for compliments. You won't get them from me.'

He laughed and swept her off her feet.

'Put me down this instant,' she exclaimed.

'Not a chance,' he said. Amusement coloured his voice. 'Don't you want to know where your adventures could take you?'

'I've got a pretty good idea, which is why I hope your tongue is firmly planted in your cheek. Just for the record, I'll be sleeping on my own tonight,' she added as Luca strode on across the courtyard with her safely locked in his arms.

'Brava,' he said, showing no sign of slowing down.

The crowd parted like the Red Sea, she noticed. She should put up some sort of token struggle, but it was a magical night, a magical moment, and not too many of them came along.

Her senses rioted when Luca dipped his head to brush a kiss against her neck. She would see this adventure through, so long as it only took her from one side of the courtyard to the other. 'I have to go,' she insisted, when he lowered her to her feet to acknowledge some boisterous partygoers.

'No. You have to stay,' he argued when he was done, and so close to her ear that it tingled.

'Are you determined to lead me astray?'

'Would I?' Sweeping her up before she had chance to protest, he strode on towards the palace gardens.

She was dangerously aroused, but for one night, she was going to be Callie from the lemon groves, without fear or guilt, or any of the dutiful thoughts that had curbed her in the past.

'Where are you taking me?' she asked as Luca opened a gate leading to lemon groves.

'Wait and see.'

He didn't stop until they reached the riverbank where he set her down. She had free will. She could do what she liked. She didn't have to do anything she didn't want to. Conscious he was watching her, she smiled, but Luca wasn't fooled. 'What's worrying you?' he said.

'I'm not worried.' Apart from the longing to have more nights like this, which she knew in her heart of hearts would not be possible. Moonlight lit the scene. Sparkling water rushed by. The bed of grass beneath her feet was soft and deep, and the midnight-blue sky overhead was littered with stars. It was the perfect setting on the perfect night, and Luca was the perfect man. Reaching out, she linked their hands.

Luca soothed and seduced her with kisses, with touches, and with the expression in his eyes. She believed they were connecting on a deeper level. He made her want to know more about him, and for this to be the start of something, rather than the grand finale. His hands worked magic on her body. His strength seduced her, his scent seduced her... everything about Luca seduced her. He was a man of the earth, a man of the people, who worked with his body, his mind, and good humour, as well as unstinting loyalty towards his Prince, which he'd proved when he had refused to point him out to her.

This adventure might have its ups and downs, but Luca had featured large in every part of it.

He made her spirit soar, and her body cry out for his touch.

They couldn't keep their hands off each other. There was no chance she was going anywhere any time soon. She was a woman with needs and desires, who saw no reason for self-denial. She hadn't prepared for this, but had taken the usual precautions, more in hope than expectation of a love life some time in the far distant future. She hadn't planned anything, because placing trust in a man was a huge deal for Callie, but Luca was different. He made her feel safe. He made her believe she could trust him.

His mouth was warm and as persuasive as sin, and, though she was tentative at first, she soon matched his fire. He was more controlled. She was not. She was new to this, and had had no idea how the fire could take hold and consume her. Luca kept his touch tantalisingly light, far too light for her frustrated body. The urge to know every part of him intimately was clawing at her senses. 'I want you,' she said as she stared up into his eyes.

He knew she was suffering. Of *course* he knew.

He was responsible for it. She was hardly playing hard to get, and Luca was available for pleasure. Tracing his magnificent torso over his insubstantial top tipped the balance from caution to action. 'Take it off,' she instructed, 'and then the rest of your clothes.'

His eyes fired with interest and amusement. 'You first,' he countered. 'Or at least, match me.'

And so the game began. It was a game with only one conclusion. Once started, it couldn't be stopped. Without breaking eye contact, she began unbuttoning her blouse. She did so slowly, and felt heat rise between them. It was her turn to make *him* wait. Pushing the soft fabric from her shoulders, she let it drop.

He frowned. 'You're wearing a bra.'

'I'd say you're overdressed too,' she murmured.

He smiled.

'You should have drawn up your rules before this started,' she teased, 'because now you have to take off your flip-flops too.'

Maintaining eye contact as he kicked them off, she whispered, 'And now your shorts.'

'Are you sure about that?'

'Absolutely sure.' She would keep her eyeline level with his.

'Take off your trainers,' he suggested.

'If that's a ruse to give me chance to have second thoughts, save it. I won't change my mind.'

'I'll take my chances.' Luca's stare was long and steady. 'By the time I've finished, you won't have a stitch of clothing on,' he promised.

She shrugged, pretending indifference, but her heart was banging in her chest. 'If you'd rather not?'

'Oh, I'd rather,' he said with a look that made her body flame with lust.

She toed off her trainers, wishing she'd dressed for the Arctic and had more clothes to remove. Luca was in serious danger of winning this game. How would such an experienced man judge her when he saw her naked? But it was exciting and fun, and every bit the adventure she'd dreamed about...the adventure she wouldn't be telling the Browns about.

She should have known he'd go commando. He'd lowered his zipper and allowed his shorts to slide down his lean frame. Currently, they were hanging on his thighs. Reaching down, he pushed them the rest of the way and, stepping out of them, he stood in front of her, unconcerned. 'You still have some way to go,' he commented.

She would not look down. 'My rules state—' She gasped as Luca yanked her close.

'Your rules count for nothing,' he assured her in a seductive growl as he nuzzled his stubble-roughened face against her neck.

'Oh—' Breath shot from her lungs. She couldn't help but rub her body against his in the hunt for more contact between them, but Luca held her firmly away.

'Not so fast,' he said, all control, while she was a gasping mass of arousal. 'I can see I have some training to do.'

'Please,' she said, making his eyes flare with amusement.

'Nice bra,' he commented as he deftly removed it.

Now that was definitely going to give him the wrong idea. She'd chosen something friv-olous for Italy. It had seemed such fun at the time. And safe. When she had been shopping in a brightly lit department store with not a single good-looking man around, the flimsy bra and thong had seemed harmless. The brand was quite exclusive, meant for show rather than practicality. Designer lingerie in bright pink silk chiffon bordered with palest aquamarine lace was hardly Callie's usual choice. She was more of a sensible white cotton type. She could only imagine what Luca was thinking.

'You're beautiful,' he murmured, reassuring and disarming her all in one breath.

'No, I'm not.'

'I guess there's only one way to convince you,' he said, laughing softly.

He drew her closer, inch by inch, and then he kissed her. And this was not a teasing brush of his lips, but something more that drew emotion out of her, until she was happy and sad, excited and confused, all at once. She was happy to be here with him, and sad because she knew it couldn't last. He excited her. Her body was going crazy for more—which he knew. And she was apprehensive too, in case she got this terribly wrong. There were *so* many ways she could get this wrong.

'Stop,' Luca murmured against her mouth. 'Stop thinking and just allow yourself to feel for once. Go with your instincts, Callie.'

Her instincts were telling her to rub herself shamelessly against him, to part her legs and find relief as quickly as she could for the throbbing ache of frustration that he'd put there. And she had mightily encouraged, Callie conceded. She wanted this badly. Even more than that, she wanted the connection between them to last, but she had to face facts: Luca was an itinerant worker, as was she, and so they'd both move on.

He kissed away her doubts as he lowered her slowly to the ground. Stretching out his length against hers on the cool swathe of grass, he made sure that the world faded away, leaving just the two of them to kiss and explore each other. It was as if time stood still. Water still bubbled nearby, and a light breeze still ruffled the leaves overhead, but they were in another world where her senses were totally absorbed in Luca's warm, clean man scent, and the feel of his powerful body against hers. His chest was shaded with just the right amount of dark hair that rasped against her nipples as he moved. She was filled with desire for him, and only felt a moment of apprehension when he reached into the pocket of his discarded shorts and she heard a foil rip. She was glad he had the good sense to protect them both, because she had no intention of pulling back. She had no regrets. None.

When he dipped his head to suckle her mind exploded with sensation. Moving her head on the cushioned earth, she bucked her hips repeatedly, involuntarily, responding to the hungry demands of her body. In the grip of sexual hunger, she reached for his shoulders and held on tightly, as if she were drowning and Luca was her rock. She had stifle a gasp of excitement when he moved over her. The weight of him against her thighs was new to her, and a little frightening. She had to tell herself that this was what she wanted, and that nothing was going to stop her now, nothing.

'I'm right here,' he soothed as if he could sense her apprehension.

'Don't I know it?' she joked half-heartedly.

'Seriously. Stop worrying. I would never hurt you.'

She stared into his eyes and saw the truth behind his statement. It was as if that had opened the floodgates to hunger, to curiosity, which left her fierce with passion, as well as uncertain as to what Luca was used to. Goodness knew, her experience was limited, to say the least. She was on a journey of discovery, Callie consoled herself, and this was an adventure that would carve a memory so deep she would never forget this moment, or this man.

Luca whispered against her mouth, 'Trust me, Callie,' and then his hands worked their magic and she was lost.

'*Oh*...that's...'

'Good?' he suggested in a low, amused murmur.

Her answer was a series of soft, rhythmical sighs. 'Better than good,' she managed to gasp.

'More?' he suggested.

The hands cupping her buttocks were so much

bigger than hers, and his skilful fingers could work all sorts of wickedness.

'Would you like me to touch you here?'

His tone was low and compelling. 'So much,' she admitted, sucking in a shaking breath.

One of Luca's slightly roughened finger pads was all it took to send her mindless with excitement. He knew exactly what to do. He started stroking steadily, rhythmically, applying the right amount of pressure at just the right speed.

'Good?'

Was she supposed to answer? She daren't speak. She was frightened of losing control.

'Would you like me to tip you over the edge?'

'I'm not sure.'

'Yes, you are.'

Staring into Luca's laughing eyes, she knew he was right.

He kissed her as he explored her, a shallow invasion at first with a single finger, and then deeper, with one, two, and finally three fingers. 'You're so ready,' he commented with approval.

She rocked her body in time to the steady thrust of Luca's hand. It wasn't as good, or as immediate as when he attended to her achingly sensitive little nub. It was a different feeling, and one just as compelling in its way. It made her want him to lodge deep inside her. The urge to be one with him was overwhelming.

Nudging her thighs apart with his, he continued to touch her in the way that took her mind off everything else. The delicious sensation of having him enclose her buttocks in his big, warm hands while he touched her lightly at the apex of her thighs was startlingly good. He found new ways to tease her, moving his body up and down until she was so aroused he could slide in easily, but then he pulled out again, provoking her more than ever. 'Don't stop!' she exclaimed with frustration.

He ignored this plea and continued to tease her. Wild for him, she begged for more in words she'd never used before.

'Like this?' Luca suggested in a low growl.

She gasped with shock when he sank deep. For a moment she didn't know if she liked it or not. He was very slow and very careful, but that only gave her chance to realise how much he stretched her. Every nerve ending she possessed leapt instantly to attention. The sensation was sudden and complete. She couldn't think, she could only feel. *'Yes,'* she sighed, moving with him.

Luca maintained a dependable rhythm, taking her to the edge and over, and he still moved intuitively, steadily, to make sure that her ride of pleasure continued for the longest possible time. She might have screamed. She might have called his name. She only knew that by the time she quietened her throat was sore, and with a gasp she collapsed back against the grass.

'And we're only just getting started,' Luca promised with amusement.

Still lodged deep, he began to move again, persuasively and gently to take account of her slowly recovering body. He kept up this sensitive buffeting until the fire gripped her again and she wound her legs tightly around his waist as he thrust deep. She didn't wait to be tipped over the edge this time, but worked her hips with his, falling fast and hard, while Luca held her firmly in place so she received the full benefit of each deep, firm stroke.

'Greedy,' he approved as she gasped for breath.

'You make me greedy.' Luca was still hard. She was still hungry. She reached for him and he took her again.

Callie was unique in his experience. It was as if they'd been lovers for years, but could enjoy the first, furious appetite that came with discovery of someone special. Not only could she match him, she fired him like no other. He was driven by the primitive urge to imprint himself on her body, her mind, and her memory. Pinning her down beneath him with her arms above her head, he thrust firmly to the hilt. She growled, and bucked towards him, as hungry as she had ever been. She was wild and abandoned, as he'd imagined Callie would be once he discovered what lay beneath her carefully cultivated shell. When they were still again, she turned towards him, as slowly as if her bones had turned to lead. Smiling, she managed groggily, 'You're amazing.'

'And so are you,' he replied softly.

CHAPTER FIVE

THEY BATHED IN the stream, seemingly unaware of the chill of the water, and dried off on the bank next to each other, kissing and staring into each other's eyes. Luca seemed surprised when she insisted she would go home on one of the staff buses, but she wasn't ready to spend the night with him. She needed to clear her head and come to terms with the fact that this might have been a life-changing experience, but it had no future.

Let this be, she thought as Luca smiled against her mouth before kissing her. Let it remain shiny and special. Allow nothing to taint it. She had those same thoughts when she boarded the bus, but by the time she walked into the hotel lobby her mood had changed, mainly because the concierge was waiting for her, and he looked worried to death.

'Thank goodness, Signorina Smith. This came for you.'

She looked at the envelope he was holding out. It was obviously urgent. She ripped it open and started reading. There was some confusion about her room at the bed and breakfast. She had intended to move hotels tomorrow, but now it seemed her room at the B & B was no longer available. Crumpling the note in her hand, she frowned as she wondered what to do next. She couldn't afford to stay on here.

'Signorina Smith?'

The concierge was hovering anxiously. 'Yes?'

'Forgive my intrusion, but I can see how concerned you are. Please don't be worried. The manager at the establishment you had hoped to move to left that note for you. He has informed us of a problem, and so it is arranged that you continue to stay here.'

Callie's cheeks flushed with embarrassment. 'I'm afraid I can't afford to stay here,' she admitted frankly. The concierge looked as embarrassed as she felt and this wasn't his fault. 'I'd love to stay on,' she added warmly. 'Everyone's been so kind to me, but I need to find somewhere cheaper. Maybe you can help?'

'Please, *signorina*,' the concierge implored, shifting uncomfortably from polished shoe to polished shoe. 'There will be no charge. You have been let down. This is a matter of local pride. The management of this hotel and the staff who care for you will be insulted if you offer payment.'

'And I'll be insulted if I don't,' Callie said bluntly. 'I really can't stay on if I don't pay my way.'

'The cost of your room has been covered.'

She swung around in surprise. 'Luca! Are you following me?'

'Yes,' he admitted.

'What do you know about this?' she demanded. Luca, tousled and magnificent, couldn't have looked more incongruous in the sleek, polished surroundings of the five-star hotel. She had to curb a smile as she glanced down at her clothes, and then at his. They both looked exactly what they were, labourers from the fields, which was another reason for decamping to another, much plainer establishment. Not that her body could have cared less what Luca was wearing. As far as her body was concerned, Luca looked better naked, anyway.

A million and one feelings flooded through her as they stared at each other. 'Are you responsible for this?' she asked, holding out the letter. Out of the corner of her eye, she could see the concierge, who'd returned to his booth, looking more anxious than ever. Something was definitely going on. Luca knew Marco. Had they pulled strings between them so that she would have to stay with Luca? She refused to be manipulated, especially by Luca.

'I couldn't help overhearing that you were having difficulties,' he began.

She bit her tongue and decided to wait to see what he said next. When he shrugged and smiled, threatening to weaken her resolve, she said, 'I don't suppose you know anything about my mysterious benefactor, or the fact that the hotel is refusing to charge me?'

He raised a brow. 'Don't you like it here?'

'That's not the point,' she insisted. It hadn't escaped her notice that Luca was speaking as calmly as if he were a tour operator dealing with a quibbling client, rather than a controlling alpha male who seemed to think that everything and everyone should run to his prescription. He might have quite literally swept her off her feet at the party, but post-party common sense had had time to set in.

'My only concern is that you have somewhere comfortable to stay,' he insisted.

She bristled. 'Well, thank you, but I'm quite capable of making my own arrangements.'

'They had a burst pipe at the small establishment where you booked a room,' Luca explained while the concierge nodded vehemently. 'Marco alerted me to this, and the concierge was only trying to help.'

'How did Marco know I was planning to move to the B & B?' she asked suspiciously.

'I'm sorry, Callie, but you can't live in a small town like this and not know what's going on.'

'So Marco told you?' How could she have been so dim?

'Stay on at the hotel,' Luca offered, as if he were the owner of the sumptuous building. 'You'll be closer to the lemon groves here.' He shot her a questioning look. 'That's if you intend to continue working on the Prince's estate.'

'Of course I do,' Callie confirmed. She loved it on the Prince's estate, and was nowhere near ready to leave yet.

'So, come back with me.'

Luca was waiting at the lobby door, as if it were all a done deal. Did he mean go back to the party with him? Or did Luca have something different in mind? She had paid for the hotel until tomorrow, and packing could wait until the morning. Meanwhile...*adventure beckoned*!

More adventure? Why not? Luca was everything virile and masculine, drawing her deeper into the adventure she'd always dreamed about. 'Thank you for your concern,' she said, knowing she needed time to think more than ever now. 'And, thank you,' she added to the concierge as she walked away.

Callie avoided him the next day. His pride was piqued. However, everyone broke for lunch in the afternoon and congregated at the cookhouse.

She was there, and they nodded to each other as they stood in line.

'Luca.'

Her greeting was cool. She hadn't appreciated his interference at the hotel, he gathered. He was hot from the fields, and hot for Callie, who had spent the morning in an air-conditioned facility the size of an aircraft hangar. Small, neat and clean, she slammed into his senses in her prim little buttoned-up blouse. Her denim shorts were short and they displayed her legs to perfection, as well as a suggestion of the curve of the bottom he'd caressed last night. That was all he needed before an afternoon's work.

'Excuse me, please,' she said politely, waiting with her loaded tray to move past him.

The urge to ruffle those smooth feathers and make her wild with passion again was more than a passing thought. Weighing up the bandana he wore tied around his head to keep his crazy hair under control, she moved on to scrutinise the ancient top skimming his waist, though was careful not to look any lower. He took charge of her tray. Her gaze settled on his hands, and then his wrists, which were banded with leather studded with semi-precious stones, collected for him by the children of Fabrizio so he wouldn't forget them while he was away. 'I can manage, thank you,' she said, trying to take the tray off him.

'I'm sure you can,' he agreed, 'but sometimes it's good to let people help you.'

Her brow pleated in thought as if she'd heard this somewhere before.

'Are you staying on at the hotel, or have you found somewhere else to stay?' he enquired lightly as he carried her tray to the table where Anita was waiting for Callie to join her.

'Is that why you're here? To question me?' Callie probed with a penetrating look.

For a moment he couldn't decide whether to shrug off her question or throw her over his shoulder like the caveman she thought him. He did know one thing. The tension between them couldn't be sustained.

'See you later,' he said, turning to go.

'Not if I see you first,' she called teasingly after him.

A little frustration would do them both good,

he decided. Ignoring the buzz of interest that accompanied him to the door, he saluted the chefs and left the cookhouse.

Infuriating man! How was it possible to feel so aroused, and yet control the impulse to jump on Luca and ravish him in front of everyone? Which was probably exactly how he expected her to feel. The tension in the cookhouse had been high, and made worse because people were obviously trying hard not to stare at them. She had tried to start a conversation with Anita, but couldn't concentrate and kept losing her train of thought.

'If you take my advice, you'll get it over with,' Anita advised, glancing at Callie with concern.

'Get what over with?' Callie demanded, frowning.

'Sex. You need to sate yourself.'

'I beg your pardon?'

'Oh, come off it, Callie. You'll be no good to anyone, least of all yourself, until you do.'

'Anita, I'm shocked!'

'No, you're not, you're frustrated,' Anita argued. 'No one would think any the worse of you if you glut yourself on that one.' She glanced in the direction Luca had gone.

'This isn't an adult playground. It's a place of work.'

'Listen to yourself,' Anita protested with a fork-ful of crisp, golden fries poised in front of her mouth. 'Take precautions and don't involve your heart. You're here for adventure, aren't you?'

It might be too late to do as Anita said, Cal-lie reflected as she left the cookhouse ahead of her friend. Her heart was already involved. She couldn't last a minute without wondering if she'd see Luca again soon.

Turning onto the dusty track leading through the lemon groves, she headed for the storage fa-cility where she'd been working that morning, only to see Luca coming towards her.

'Shall I show you a short cut?' he offered.

A short cut to what? she wondered as he grinned and took hold of her hand.

It was no good. He couldn't get through the af-ternoon without it, without her, without Callie, without being up against a tree kissing her as if they were the last couple on earth and time was running out fast.

'Luca—we can't—'

'Yes, we can,' he insisted. Pressing his body weight against her, he slowly moved his body against hers until she was sucking in great gulping sobs of frustration.

'I need you,' she gasped out.

'I know,' he whispered.

He found her with his hand over the rough, thick denim shorts and stroked firmly. He could feel her heat and his imagination supplied the rest. He couldn't wait. Neither could she. They tore at her shorts together. Removing them quickly, he tossed them away. There was no time for kissing, or touching, or preparing, there was only this. He freed himself. She scrambled up him. He dipped at the knees and took her deep. She came violently after a few firm thrusts. Tearing at him with hands turned to claws, she threw back her head and howled out her pleasure as each powerful spasm gripped her. When he felt her muscles relax, and her hands lost their grip, he gave it to her again, fast and hard.

'Yes!' she cried out as he claimed her again. 'More,' she begged, blasting a fiercely demanding stare into his eyes.

'You can have all you want,' he promised as he worked her steadily towards the next release. 'But not right now,' he murmured, still thrusting, 'because we have to go back to work.'

'You're joking.' Her eyes widened. 'How can I go back to work after this?'

'That discipline we talked about?'

'*You* talked about.'

He ended the argument with a few fast thrusts, and she screamed out her pleasure as they both claimed their most powerful release yet.

'You're right,' she accepted groggily a long while after she'd quietened. 'They'll be short a team member if I don't go back, and I can't let everyone down.'

He could have sorted this out for her with a few words in the appropriate ear, but that would be taking advantage of his position, and so he huffed an accepting laugh and lowered her down to the ground. They were both bound by duty. Groping for his phone, he clicked it on to see the time. What he saw was a line of missed calls. Springing up, he dislodged her. 'Sorry, I have to take this,' he explained as he walked away. Sorting himself out as the call connected, he tucked the phone between ear and his shoulder and asked a few pertinent questions. Having cut the line, he beckoned to Callie. 'Sorry, but there's somewhere I have to be.'

'Your afternoon shift?' she queried, frowning.

'Something like that, but I'll have to leave the estate.'

'Is there anything I can do to help?' she asked, feeling his tension.

'Nothing.' He sounded abrupt, but there was no time for explanations.

Callie was hurt. She refused to meet his eyes. His sharp response had shocked her. And no wonder, when one minute they were totally absorbed in each other, even if that was up against a tree, and the next he couldn't wait to leave. It couldn't be helped. He'd see her again, if and when he came back.

* * *

She didn't have much experience of love affairs, but she knew enough to know Luca's behaviour wasn't acceptable. His intended departure was brutal and sudden, and only went to prove she didn't know the man she was with. She didn't know him at all. Shame and humiliation swept over her in hot, ugly waves as he paced impatiently while she struggled to put on her shorts as fast as she could. For Luca it was just sex, necessary like eating and breathing, and now it was done, he couldn't wait to leave.

What a mug I am, Callie thought as she pulled up her zipper. Even her well-used body mocked her as she dressed. It was so tender and still so responsive, while her mind continued to whirl in agitated spirals as she flashed glances at a man who seemed to have forgotten she existed. She'd been swept up in a fantasy, but as far as Luca was concerned they were two healthy adults who'd wanted sex. Now that was done there was nothing left. She couldn't even be angry with him. She'd been a more than willing partner. She was just puzzled as to how they could seem so close, and now this.

She glanced at him. He glanced back, but only to check on her progress. There'd be no more conversation or confiding, no more intimate jokes. Smoothing her hair as best she could, she looked at the time on her phone and grimaced. She was already late for the afternoon shift and would have to take a shower before returning to work. It must have been her heavy sigh that prompted Luca to say, 'There are facilities next to the building where you're working. You'll find everything there—towels, shampoo—'

Did he do this on a regular basis? Callie wondered. 'Thanks.' Why wouldn't he? Luca came here every year. She couldn't be the first woman to fall for his blistering charm. Her face flamed red as she pictured him with someone else. She'd thought they were special, which only went to prove how little she knew about men. She could understand he was in a hurry, but couldn't there be just the slightest pleasantry between them, to allow for an exit with dignity?

'So that's it?' she said as she checked her top was properly tucked in.

'Should there be more?' he demanded.

His response was the slap in the face she badly needed. Something had to bring her to her senses. Reality had landed. Hooray. He was right. What more should there be?

Callie was angry, but they were hardly at the stage where he could confide state secrets. She controlled herself well, but the tension in her jaw and the spark in her eyes told their own story. It couldn't be helped. News of Max's attempted coup was for his ears only. He strode on ahead as soon as Callie was ready. His mind was already elsewhere. Stabbing numbers into his cell, he told his staff to prepare the helicopter. He had to get to Fabrizio fast. He would just have time to shower and change before it arrived to pick him up. Max and his cronies had been causing trouble again, and, though they had been swiftly suppressed, the people of Fabrizio needed the reassurance of seeing their Prince.

'So, you're not even going to wait for me?' Callie called after him.

He turned around, shrugged impatiently then kept on walking. She was no longer his priority. However much he might want her to be, he couldn't put his own selfish pleasures first.

'What's got under your skin?' Anita asked when the two women bumped into each other outside the shower block. 'A man? One man in particular?'

Anita sounded so hopeful that Callie couldn't bear to disillusion her. 'Tell you later,' she promised as she hurried off for her afternoon shift.

'Wave goodbye to the Prince before you go,' Anita called after her.

Callie stopped and turned around. 'Where is he?'

Shielding her eyes, Anita stared up at a large blue helicopter with a royal crest of Fabrizio on the side.

'Apparently he's been called back to Fabrizio to deal with an emergency,' Anita explained as both women protected their eyes against the aircraft's downdraft, which had raised dust clouds all around them. 'Don't worry. It won't be an emergency when Luca gets there.'

'Sorry?' Callie froze.

'Prince Luca's will is stronger than any army his brother Max could raise, *and* his people adore him,' Anita explained. 'The people don't trust Max as far as they could throw him. I read in the press today that Prince Luca intends to buy Max off. Max will do anything for money,' Anita explained, 'and that includes relinquishing his claim to the throne. Max needs Luca's money to pay his gambling debts. He'd bleed the country dry, if he became ruler. The late Prince, their father, knew this. That's why he made Prince Luca his heir—Callie? Are you all right?'

'Why didn't you tell me that Luca was the Prince?' Callie stared at her friend in total disbelief, but how could she be angry with Anita when Callie was guilty of ignoring what had been, quite literally, under her nose?

'I'm sorry,' Anita said as she enveloped Callie in a big hug. 'I thought you knew. I thought, like the rest of us, you were being discreet by not naming him, or talking about him. We all know that's what Prince Luca prefers. If I'd guessed for a moment—'

'It's not your fault,' Callie insisted. 'I'm to blame. I only saw what I wanted to see.' She stared up at the helicopter as it disappeared behind some cloud. Luca hadn't told her anything, let alone that he was the Prince. What a fool she was. How could she have missed all the clues? They were as obvious to her now as the bright red arrow she hadn't noticed when she'd first arrived at the Prince's estate. Only worse, much worse, Callie concluded. She didn't blame Luca. Was he supposed to act like Prince Charming in a fairy tale? He was a man, with all the cravings, faults and appetite that went along with that, and she hadn't exactly fought him off.

'Why are you laughing?' Anita asked.

Callie was thinking that Luca didn't have to excuse his actions. He simply called for his helicopter and flew off. But into a difficult situation, she reminded herself. Even if Luca and his brother had never been close, no one needed to remind Callie how much a barb from within the family could hurt.

'I thought he was one of us,' she admitted to Anita.

'He is one of us,' Anita confirmed hotly.

Callie smiled, knowing there was no point in arguing with Anita, one of Luca's staunchest supporters, but she still couldn't get her head around her own clumsy mistake. It was so much easier to think of Luca as a worker, rather than a prince, but how she could have been so wrapped up in her Italian adventure that she hadn't guessed the truth before now defeated her.

'Max's uprising was over before it began,' Anita explained as she linked arms with Callie. 'You can't fault Prince Luca for keeping his word to his father, the late Prince. Luca's been coming here for years to work alongside the pickers, but nothing's more important to him than the pledge he made to keep his country safe, and we all understand why he had to go back to Fabrizio.'

All except Callie, who was still floundering about in the dark wondering why Luca hadn't told her his true identity. Perhaps there were too many people who only wanted to be close to him for the benefits they could gain, apparently like his brother, Max. She could forgive him if that were the case. Well, sort of. Luca expected her to trust him, but he clearly didn't trust her.

And was she always truthful?

The only time she'd reached out since arriving in Italy was to text Rosie to reassure the Browns that everything was going well. She'd explained that she was going to extend her stay, but had kept her answers to Rosie's excited questions bland in the extreme. She was staying on because she wanted to learn more about Italy, Callie had said, which explained why she had taken a part-time job. She just hadn't expected to get her heart broken into pieces and trampled on in the process. 'I'll be leaving soon,' she mused out loud.

'Must you? Oh, no. Please don't. Was it something I said? I didn't mean to probe,' Anita assured Callie with concern, 'and I'll understand completely if you don't want to tell me why you're leaving.'

Callie responded with a warm hug for her new friend. 'You've done nothing wrong,' she assured Anita. 'If anyone's at fault, it's me. I could have asked Luca more questions, but chose not to. I didn't want reality to intrude, I suppose. It's better if I go home and get real. It's too easy to believe the dream here.'

How true was that? She couldn't believe she'd made such a fool of herself with Luca.

'Can't you stay a little longer?' Anita begged. 'We're only just getting to know each other, and I'll miss you.'

Tears sprang to Callie's eyes at this confession, and the two women exchanged a quick, fierce hug. 'I hope you'll come and visit me?' Callie insisted. 'I don't want to lose touch, either.'

'No chance,' Anita promised stoutly as they stood side by side on the dusty path that ran through the groves. 'When I go home, it's to a damp northern mill town not too far from your docks, so there's no reason why we can't meet up.'

'Come for Christmas,' Callie exclaimed impetuously. 'Please. I'll ask Ma Brown. The more, the merrier, she always says. Promise you will.'

'Are you serious?' Anita looked concerned, and then her face lit up when she realised that

Callie meant every word. 'I usually spend Christmas alone.'

'Not this year,' Callie vowed passionately with another warm hug. 'I'll speak to Ma and Pa Brown as soon as I get back, and I'll send you the details.'

'You're a true friend, Callie,' Anita said softly.

'I won't forget you,' Callie promised.

Casting one last wistful look around the sun-drenched lemon groves, Callie firmed her jaw. She might be Callie from the docks when she returned home, but she would always be Callie from the lemon groves in her heart.

CHAPTER SIX

'WHERE THE HELL is she? Someone must know.'

The staff stared at him blankly. He was back in the warehouse where the lemons were stored. As soon as he'd sorted the problems in Fabrizio, he'd returned to his estate expecting to find Callie still working there. He hadn't realised how much he'd miss her until she wasn't around. 'Callie Smith?' he exclaimed, exasperated by the continued silence. 'Anyone?'

Apologetic shrugs greeted his questions. No one knew where she was. Or they weren't telling, he amended, glancing at Anita, who was staring fixedly six inches above his head. He'd made it back just before the end of the season when the casual workers left. Most of the pickers had already gone home, but some had stayed on to make sure everything was stored properly and they were set fair for next year. *Why would Callie stay when I've been so brusque?*

Wheeling around, he strode to the exit. Fresh from resolving a potential uprising in Fabrizio, he could surely solve the mystery of one missing woman. Max had accepted a pay-off equivalent to the GDP of a small country, and Luca had paid this gladly with the proviso that Max stayed out of Luca's life and never returned to Fabrizio. He had the funds to buy anything he wanted, even freedom from Max, but could he buy Callie? In the short time he'd known her, he'd learned that, not only was Callie irreplaceable, she was unpredictable too. Her newfound freedom after years of duty to her father had lifted her, and in the space of a couple of days Luca had succeeded in knocking her down. Throwing money at a problem like Max worked. Callie was just as likely to throw it back.

He entered the office on the estate and everyone stood to attention. In a dark, tailored suit, Luca was dressed both as a prince and a billionaire, and not one member of staff had missed that change. 'Relax, please. I'm here to ask for your help.'

As always, his people couldn't have been more accommodating. They gave him Callie's home address from her file. Now there was just Callie to deal with, he reflected as he left the building. He doubted she'd be quite so helpful, and his smile faded. He'd never been unsure of an outcome before, but he couldn't be sure of Callie.

He took the helicopter for the short flight to the airport, where his flight plan to the north of England was already filed. He'd fly the jet himself. The thought of being a passenger appalled him. He needed something to do. Callie occupied every corner of his mind. The unfinished business between them banged at his brain. There was no time to lose. He didn't leave loose ends, never had.

Could it really be more than two months since she'd first met Luca? It was certainly time to take stock of her life. That didn't take very long. She was living in one freezing, cold room over a dress shop where she worked six days a week to fund her studies at night school. She was determined to get ahead by building on the Italian language she'd already picked up on her trip to Italy. Her love affair with the country was in no way over, and it had turned out that she had a flair for languages. She had moved to another town, because she didn't have a home to go back to as such. Her old home next door to the Browns had new tenants, and though the Browns had begged her to stay on with them, Callie had insisted that they'd done enough for her, and that it was time for her to go it alone. 'I wish I could have brought you more exciting news from my adventures,' she'd told them.

'Exciting enough,' Rosie had exclaimed, her eyes fever bright when Callie talked about the Prince.

Callie hadn't told anyone about the time she'd spent locked in the Prince's arms, and had deflected Rosie's questions by telling her that staying in a five-star hotel had kept her away from the real Italy. 'The posh hotel was lovely,' she'd explained, 'but it was bland.'

'Unlike the Italian men?' Rosie guessed, still digging for information.

'And so I looked for a job amongst the people,' Callie had driven on in an attempt to avoid Rosie's question. She had never lied to her friend, and she never would.

'You're too hard on yourself, love,' Pa Brown had insisted when Callie explained that without the young maid's suggestion she would still have been sitting in the hotel, rather than experiencing the lemon groves she had grown to love. 'You wanted to get out and do an honest day's work. You asked for help to find some. There's nothing wrong with that. We all need help sometimes.'

Pa Brown's words resonated with Callie more than ever now. He was right. In her current situation, she would have to ask for help at some point.

Yes. From Callie Smith, Callie concluded. Like millions of women who'd found themselves in this situation, she'd get through, and get through well. Though there were times when she wished she'd agreed to see Luca when he first flew to England to set things straight between them.

'Why won't you see him?' Rosie had asked

with incredulity on the first occasion. 'He's an incredible man and he cares about you. He must do, to leave everything to fly here to find you. And he's a prince, Cal,' Rosie had added in an awestruck gasp, 'as well as one of the richest men in the world.'

Callie remembered firming her lips and refusing to add to this in any way. She had simply given her head a firm shake. The money meant nothing to her and neither did Luca's title. She couldn't risk her heart being broken again, and the feelings she had for Luca were so strong they frightened her. But Rosie knew her too well. Realising Callie wouldn't change her mind, Rosie had put an arm around Callie's shoulders and hugged her tight. 'I know you love him,' Rosie insisted. 'And one day you'll know that too. Just don't find out when it's too late.'

It hadn't ended there, of course. Luca wasn't the type to meekly turn around and go home. He didn't know how to take no for an answer. He'd called several times, sent flowers, gifts, notes, hampers of dainty cakes and delicacies from a famous London store. He'd even despatched an elderly statesman called Michel to plead his case. Callie had felt particularly bad about the old man, but Ma Brown had made up for her refusal, treating Michel to a real northern afternoon tea before politely telling him that his Prince had no chance of changing Callie's mind at the moment. 'You shouldn't even have given him that much hope,' Callie had insisted. 'I don't want to be any man's mistress and Luca's a prince. He's hardly going to take things in the direction I...'

As her voice had tailed away, Pa Brown had piped up, 'The direction you want is love, Callie. Love and respect is the direction you're entitled to want, when you give your heart to someone special.'

As Ma Brown had sighed with her romantic heart all aflutter, Callie had known it was time to move on. Her relationship with Luca, such as it had been, had started to affect the Browns, so she'd told them what she planned to do, and had packed her bags. And here she was three months later in Blackpool, the jewel of the Fylde coast. It was blustery and cold this close to Christmas, but there was an honest resilience about the place that suited Callie's mood. And there were the illuminations, she mused with a rueful grin as she glanced out of her top-floor window at the light-bedecked seafront. Known as the greatest free light show on earth, one million bulbs and six miles of lights brought tourists flocking, which meant there were plenty of part-time jobs.

The irony since she'd been here was that Luca was never out of the press. She couldn't believe she'd spent so much time in blissful ignorance as to his identity when his face stared out of every magazine and newspaper. Even when she went to the hairdresser's, she couldn't escape him. She had read every column inch written about him, and knew now that Luca had won his position in Fabrizio thanks to his sheer grit and determination. That, and the love of an adoptive father who had always believed his 'boy from the gutters of Rome', as Luca was referred to in the red-tops, was an exceptional man in the making.

Callie had become an expert in press releases and could quote some of them by heart. Luca, who was already a titan in business, was now equally respected in diplomatic circles. A tireless supporter of good causes, he had just completed a world tour of the orphanages he sponsored.

The photos of him were riveting. Luca relaxing, looking hot as hell in snug-fitting jeans, or Luca riding a fierce black stallion, looking like the king of the world. He could be cool and strong on state occasions, when he was easily the most virile and commanding of all the men present. In a nutshell, the new ruler of Fabrizio currently dominated world news, which made him seem further away to Callie, and more unreachable than ever. Much was made in the press of his lonely bachelor status, but Luca clearly had no intention of changing that any time soon. Flowers arrived regularly at the Browns', a clear indication that he hadn't given up his search for a mistress yet.

The flowers were still arriving, Rosie had informed Callie only last night, together with the handwritten letters bearing the royal seal, which Rosie had insisted on squirrelling away for Callie. 'You'll look at them one day,' she'd said, not realising that Callie steamed them open and had read every one.

She'd never fit into Luca's glitzy life, Callie concluded, however much affection and humour he put into his letters. But there were deeper reasons. Her mother had died believing her father's lies, and Callie had listened to them for most of her life. 'Tomorrow will be better,' Callie's father would promise each day. But it was never better. He always gambled away the money, or drank it, and so Callie would do another shift at the pub. Did she want another man who lied to her, even if not telling her that he was a prince was a lie of omission by Luca to test how genuine she was? She would be the one lying if she couldn't admit to herself that each time she saw a photograph of Luca, she longed for him with all her heart.

'The trick is knowing when to say thank you, and get on with things,' Pa Brown had told her in their last telephone conversation, when Callie had asked what she should do about the flowers. 'You can send us your thank-you notes, and we'll pass them on. Don't you worry, our Callie, Ma Brown's loving it. She's like Lady Bountiful, spreading those flowers around the neighbourhood so they do some good. You can thank that Prince Luca properly when you see him in person. I certainly will.'

We won't be seeing him, Callie had wanted to say, but she didn't have the heart.

'Stop beating yourself up, girl,' Pa Brown had added before they ended their most recent call. 'You went to work in the lemon groves, which was what you'd dreamed about. You turned that dream into reality, which is more than most of us do.'

She should have kept a grip on reality when it came to Luca, Callie thought with a sigh. But she hadn't. She had allowed herself to be swept up in the fantasy of a holiday romance. And now there was something else she had to do, something far more important than fretting. Reaching into her tote, she pulled out the paper chemist's bag. She couldn't put the test off any longer. While her periods had always been irregular this was a big gap, even for her. Now, she had to know. It was a strange thing, becoming pregnant, Ma Brown had told Callie before the last baby Brown was born. There could be barely any signs for a doctor to detect, but a mother knew. For a couple of weeks now Callie had tried to believe that this was an old wives' tale, but she couldn't kid herself any longer. She might not be a mother, or have personal experience of becoming pregnant, but she did know when she wasn't alone in her body and there was a new, fragile life to protect. She had considered that this feeling might possibly be nothing more than the product of an overactive imagination. There was only one way to find out.

She stared at the blue line unblinking. Not because if she stared long enough it might disappear, but because she was filled with the sort of euphoria that only came very rarely in life. It was a moment to savour before reality kicked in, and she was going to close her eyes and enjoy every moment of it. When she opened them again, her biggest fear was that the kit was faulty. Surely, there had to be a percentage that were?

Leaning forward, she turned on another bar of the ancient electric fire and pulled the cheap throw that usually covered the holes in the sofa around her shoulders as she tried to stop shivering. Part of that was excitement, she supposed, though her hands were frozen. She couldn't believe it was December next week. Where had the time gone? It only seemed five minutes since she had been basking in sunshine in Italy. That was almost three months ago. Three months of life-shattering consequence, Callie reflected as she stared, and stared again at the blue line on her pregnancy test. One thing was certain. She'd have to see Luca now.

He knew Callie was pregnant since he'd tracked her down to England. He'd been tied up with his enthronement once the dispute with Max was settled. That stiff and formal ceremony was over now, with the celebratory garden party for thousands of citizens of Fabrizio still to come. He loved being amongst his people and looked forward to it, but it was time to concentrate on Callie. They were similar in so many ways, which warned him to tread carefully, or Callie would only back off more determinedly than ever. And hormones would be racing, so the mother of his child, the one woman he could never forget, would have more fire in her than a volcano. Once more into the breach, he thought as the royal jet, piloted by His Serene Highness, Luca Fabrizio, the most frustrated and most determined man on earth, soared high into the air.

Blackpool Illuminations Requires Tour Guides. Callie studied the headline. She was going to need more money soon. Her bank account was bouncing along the bottom, and when the baby arrived... Touching her stomach, she was filled with wonder at the thought; when the baby arrived there would be all sorts of expenses. A wave of regret swept over her, at the knowledge Luca should be part of this. The sooner she told him, the better, but he must understand she didn't want anything from him.

But the baby might need things.

Might need the father she'd never really had, Callie mused, frowning. But what would that mean? Would Luca be a good father? Instinct said yes, but would he and his royal council control their every move? What about the lack of freedom that being royal would mean for a child?

She wrapped her arms protectively around her stomach as, hot on the heels of excited disbelief and the marvel of a new life, came a very real fear of the unknown. What if she was a hopeless mother?

She couldn't afford to be frightened of anything, Callie concluded with a child on the way. Grabbing her coat and scarf, she quickly put them on. Leaving the bedsit, she locked the door behind her. The baby came before everything. She had to make some money, even save a little, so she could move to somewhere bigger, hopefully somewhere with a garden. Long before that, she had to buy clothes and equipment for the baby.

Remembering not to rattle down the stairs at a rate of knots as she usually did, she walked sensibly, thinking about the baby. She was already feeling protective. She was confident of one thing. She would not be separated from her child. Luca would have to know they were expecting a baby but, Prince or not, billionaire or not, she would not allow him, or his council, to take over. She would raise her child to have values and warmth, and teach it to be kind. The

Browns would help. Maybe she'd have to move back to the docks, but not yet. Burying her face in her scarf to protect it from the bitter wind, she prepared to brave the weather to find a job.

And Luca?

He was an Italian male. Of course he'd want to be part of this. But he would also want to found a dynasty, and for that he needed a princess, not Callie from the docks.

She exchanged a cheery hello with the kindly shop owner who had rented Callie the flat and paused to help with a string of tinsel. 'Thank you, darling,' the elderly shop owner exclaimed, giving Callie a warm hug. 'I can't believe how you're glowing. You look wonderful. Don't you get cold outside, now.'

'I won't,' Callie called back over her shoulder as she stepped out into the street.

He saw the car coming from the end of the street. Driven at speed, it was being chased by a police vehicle, sirens blaring.

No!

He wasn't sure if he shouted, or thought the

warning, but he did know he moved. Sprinting like a cheetah, he hurtled down the road. Shoving pedestrians from the path of the car, his sightline fixed on his goal. Time remained frozen, or so it seemed to him, with countless variables of horror possible.

Most people hadn't even realised there was a problem. Callie was one of them. She was still walking across the street, oblivious to the danger hurtling towards her. Launching himself at her, he slammed her to the ground. There was a thump, a screech of brakes, and for a moment the world went black, then the woman in his arms, the woman he had cushioned from the edge of the pavement with his body, battled to break free.

'Are you okay?' she exclaimed with fierce concern, lifting herself up to stare at him.

Winded, he was only capable of a grunt. She stared at him in disbelief. 'Luca?'

He gulped in a lungful of fumes and dust, mixed with Callie's warm fragrance, then, as his brain clicked back into gear, he had only one concern, and that was Callie. 'Are you hurt?'

'No.' She hesitated. 'At least, I don't think so.'

Colour drained from her face. He could imagine the thoughts bombarding her brain. She was pregnant. Was the baby okay? Could she reel back the clock and walk across the road a few seconds later or sooner? Did she have any pain? She squeezed her eyes tightly shut, making him think she was examining her body, searching for signs of trauma, particularly in her womb. She slowly relaxed, which he took to be a good sign. And then she remembered him. He saw the recognition and surprise in her eyes turn to suspicion and anger, and then back again, when she remembered where they were and how they had got there.

'You saved me,' she breathed.

'Grazie Dio!' he murmured.

Her gaze hardened again. *He* was back. The man she had thought she knew had turned out to be someone else entirely. She'd flirted with him, and had had sex with a man she had believed to be an itinerant field worker, who had turned out to be a billionaire prince, and an important figure on the world stage. He could imagine her affront when she'd found out. It wouldn't have taken her long. Settling back into her normal life, she could hardly avoid seeing his face in the press after his enthronement. In shock, she would be trying to process every piece of information, amongst which had to be what the hell was he doing here?

He followed her gaze as she glanced around to see if anyone else was hurt. He saw the tyre marks on the pavement left by the car as it had mounted the kerb, and realised how kind fate had been. Pockets of survivors were checking each other out. Numbers were being exchanged and arms thrown around complete strangers. This was human nature at its best. From what he could see, everyone was shaken up, but thankfully unharmed. Quite a crowd had gathered. People were calling on their phones. The emergency services would arrive soon. The police were already on the scene. The youth behind the wheel of the speeding car had been captured. Patrol cars had his vehicle boxed in.

'Luca,' Callie gritted out, managing to fill that single word with all the bitterness and uncertainty prompted by his supposed deception. When she was calm, she might realise they'd both been escaping their normal lives during their time in the lemon groves. Both had seized the chance to escape and explore a different, looser version of themselves. But none of that mattered now. All that mattered was that Callie was safe. However, she, understandably, took a rather different view. 'I can't believe this,' she said, staring at him. 'What are you doing here?'

Ignoring her understandable surprise, he concentrated on essentials. 'Take it easy. Slowly,' he advised as she struggled to sit up. 'You might feel dizzy for a while. You've had a shock.'

'To put it mildly,' she agreed. 'Are you all right?' she asked tensely.

'Don't worry about me.'

'You came down with quite a bang.'

He wasn't interested in discussing anything but Callie, and was only relieved that he'd reached her in time.

'Sorry.' She started to giggle. Hysteria, he guessed. 'But we must stop meeting like this.'

He couldn't agree more. They were lying in the road on a bed of grime and oil patches. Hoping that laughter signified her body's resilience to the blow it had just received, he huffed wryly, and for a moment they weren't at loggerheads, but just two people caught up in an unexpected incident on a cold and wintry street.

'Oh, no!' Callie was staring at the stolen vehicle, which was planted in what appeared to be a dress shop window. 'My landlady,' she exclaimed, starting to get up.

'Let me help you.'

She pushed him away in panic. 'I have to make sure she's all right.'

'You have to get checked out first,' he argued.

'What *are* you doing here?' she demanded as he shrugged off his jacket and draped it around her shoulders.

'You're in shock, Callie. You need to go to hospital for a check-up now.'

'I'm fine,' she insisted, starting to pull his jacket off.

He closed it around her. 'You're shivering. You're in shock,' he repeated, 'and until the paramedics get here and check you out, I'm not taking any chances.'

'So you freeze to death instead?'

'I don't think it will come to that,' he soothed, 'do you? I'm just glad I got here when I did. I couldn't get here any sooner.'

'I heard you'd been busy,' she admitted.

A paramedic interrupted them. 'You all right, love?' he asked, proffering a foil blanket. 'Let the gentleman have his jacket back, or he'll catch his death of cold.'

'I've been trying to give it back to him,' Callie explained, 'but he won't take it.'

'Well, if he's happy for you to keep it.' The paramedic shrugged as he arranged the foil blanket over the jacket for extra warmth. 'Not too many gallant gentlemen left, love,' he commented. 'Better hang onto this one.'

Callie hummed and smiled, though Luca wondered if her smile was for the paramedic's benefit. 'Was anyone else hurt?' she asked. 'The lady in the dress shop?'

'Had just gone to make herself a cup of tea,' the paramedic reassured her. 'She was working in the shop window, she told me, only minutes before the car struck.'

'What a relief,' Callie gasped. 'I was with her. I live over the shop,' she explained.

'It's thanks to the quick thinking of your knight in shining armour that a young mother and her baby were also shoved to safety and saved from injury. He's a real hero. Aren't you, sir?'

'I wouldn't say that.' Luca had acted on instinct. There had been no planning involved. There'd been no time to think. He'd done what was necessary to avert disaster, in his view, and that was all.

'Accept praise when it's due, sir. You're a genuine hero, sir,' the paramedic assured him. 'Now, excuse me, miss, but we'd better get you to hospital for a check-up. If the gentleman wants to come too—'

'He doesn't want to come,' Callie said with a glance his way. 'You obviously know where I live,' she added, narrowing her eyes, 'so we'll speak later.'

Shepherding her to one of the two waiting ambulances, the paramedic steadied her as she climbed inside. 'What are you doing?' Callie demanded when he swung in behind her.

'Collecting my jacket?' Luca suggested dryly.

The paramedic gave him a broad wink, but had the good sense to appear busy with paperwork when the doors closed and the ambulance set off. Callie disapproved of him accompanying her to the hospital. Too bad. As she had been a member of his staff, he had a duty of care towards her, and with a baby on the horizon that duty had doubled.

'You saved her, mate,' the paramedic put in as he settled down.

This wasn't how he'd pictured his reunion with Callie. He just wanted her to be safe.

'Have you been spying on me?' Callie asked, careful not to let their companion hear her conversation.

He shrugged. He wasn't going to lie. It was a fine line between his security team's protection service and overstepping the mark. 'Your welfare and that of our child is my only concern.'

She blenched. He didn't think he'd ever seen anyone so pale. 'Are you all right? Pain? You're not—'

'No. At least, I don't think so.' Her eyes were

wide with fear as she stared at him. She reached for his hand. For the first time, she looked vulnerable. This was a very different woman from the Callie he'd met in Italy. This was a woman afraid for her unborn child, and discovering she cared for that child far more than she cared for herself. 'Don't,' she said. 'Don't look at me like that.'

'Like what?'

'As if I'm special and you're glad you're here.'

'You are special. You're about to become a mother, the mother of my child. And if I am looking at you, it's only because you're covered in grit and filth and need a good wash.'

'Charming, mate,' the paramedic piped up, proving that he wasn't lost in his work after all. 'Which charm school did you attend?'

'I didn't go to school until I was ten,' Luca admitted wryly. 'And then it was the school of hard knocks.'

'Hey, wait a minute,' the paramedic exclaimed, turning to stare at Luca intently. 'Aren't you that billionaire bloke who started life in the gutters of Rome and became a prince?' And when Luca didn't reply, he added, 'What are you doing in Blackpool?'

He winked at Callie. 'I've been checking out a new set of gutters, mate.'

'Don't you worry,' the paramedic told Callie. 'I won't tell a soul. And you're going to be okay, love, we'll make sure of that.'

The atmosphere lightened a little, and Callie didn't resist when Luca put his arm around her and drew her close.

CHAPTER SEVEN

LUCA WAS BACK. Callie's mind was in turmoil, and as for her heart… What a time for him to choose to come back! The best time, she conceded gratefully as the ambulance raced towards the hospital. She knew shock was playing a part in her mixed-up feelings, but on top of the accident and Luca returning to find her, and above all the fear that her recent fall had harmed the baby, her thoughts were spinning around and around.

'Okay?'

Had she really believed that putting distance between them would lessen her feelings for him? This wasn't the Amalfi coast where she could make the excuse of her senses being heightened by sunlight and laughter, but a grey northern coastal town in winter, and yet Luca was as compelling as ever.

'Hey,' he whispered. 'You're safe now.'

His arms seemed designed to protect. They had certainly protected Callie when she'd needed him. And now Luca's embrace was sending a very different kind of shiver spinning down her spine.

'Look at me,' he whispered. 'I said, you're safe.'

Even with his hair tousled and grazes down one side of his face, Luca looked what he was: a hero, her hero. When they'd first met it had been lust at first sight for Callie, but now it was something much more.

'Callie?'

Instinctively nursing her still-flat stomach, as if to protect the child inside, she stared into Luca's eyes.

'We're here,' he explained gently. 'We've arrived at the hospital.'

'Oh...'

The paramedic stood aside as Luca helped her down from the ambulance. She clutched the foil blanket tighter as the wind whipped around her shoulders. The only part of her that felt warm was her hand in Luca's. His grip was warm and strong, and it was with reluctance that she broke free from him in the screened-off cubicle when a doctor came to check her over.

'I want an exhaustive examination. Whatever it costs,' Luca emphasised.

'She'll have the best of care,' the doctor assured him. 'We'll be careful that nothing escapes our notice.'

'She's pregnant.'

Luca knew everything. He probably had a drone positioned over the house. But when he thanked the doctor and turned around, she could only feel warm and thankful that he was back.

He was unharmed and impatient to leave, but first he had to make absolutely sure that Callie was okay. He'd wait as long as it took. Mud spattered his clothes. His jeans were ripped. Every bit of exposed skin had taken a battering. The nurses wanted to treat his wounds, but all he cared about was Callie. He sat outside the exam room while she was put through various tests. They were both ecstatic at the outcome. Babies in the womb were surprisingly well protected against trauma, the doctor told them both, and Callie had got off lightly with a sprained ankle and a colourful selection of scrapes and bruises. Apart from the shock, she was fine and could go home. The medical staff had been superb at every stage. He showed his gratitude with a generous donation, which was very well received.

'And now for your bath,' he told Callie as he escorted her off the hospital premises.

'My bath?' she queried, looking at him in bemusement.

'Yes.' They'd cleaned up her minor injuries in the emergency room, but like him she was still covered in dirt from the road, and he had plans. A short drive to the airport would be followed by a flight to his superyacht where Callie could enjoy a rest at sea. Heading south to the sun would be the perfect remedy, allowing her to chill out in privacy while they discussed the future.

'I can have a bath at home,' she said. 'Leave me here. I'll take a cab. Thanks for all you've done—'

'You will not take a cab,' he assured her. 'You

can play tough all you like, Callie Smith, but the rules changed when you got pregnant.'

'It took two for me to get pregnant,' she reminded him.

'Which is why I'm prescribing rest for you.'

She gave him a look and then pulled out her phone.

'What are you doing?'

'Calling my landlady to check she's okay, and calling a cab. And guess what,' she added after a few moments of conversation with someone on the other end of the line. 'Turns out an unknown fairy godmother has waved a magic wand, so builders and window fitters are already on site at my landlady's shop, securing the building. I don't suppose you'd know anything about that?'

'Fairy godfather, please.'

She hummed and gave him a look.

'About that cab,' he said.

'Please respect my independence, Luca.'

'I do,' he assured her.

'Anywhere *I* want to go could easily turn into wherever you plan for me to go, and I need to get used to you being back first.'

He had no answer for that. She was right.

'Are you going to log my every move?' she asked with a welcome return of her customary good humour.

'Only some of them,' he said straight-faced.

'My lift is on its way,' she said. 'Give me a chance to think things through. It's all been such a shock. And I don't just mean the accident. Finding out your true identity, and then the months we've spent apart. The gifts you sent. The notes you wrote.'

'Would it have been easier if I hadn't contacted you?'

A brief flash of pain in her eyes said it would have been hell. The same went for him.

'I knew we had to talk when I discovered I was having your baby. I would never leave you in the dark. I just need time to process everything that's happened today. Just the fact that your security team has been watching me is unnerving. I realise you're a prince and I'm having your child, but that doesn't give you the right to put me under surveillance.'

'Your safety will always be my concern.'

'Just don't let it become your obsession.'

'My security team check out anyone I'm seen with. They report to me, and I can hardly avoid reading what they put in their reports.'

'I accept that,' she said, 'and I thank you for being so honest with me. And most especially for saving my life,' she added in a softer tone.

'I don't want your thanks. I want your time.' He was impatient for a very good reason. The royal council was pressing him to find a bride. The country was waiting. He needed an heir, and Callie's pregnancy had set a clock ticking. He needed things settled between them before the ticking stopped.

'You left me without an explanation, Luca, and now you're back I'm supposed to snap to attention?'

'I never misled you.'

'You never told me you were a prince, either,' Callie pointed out. 'You allowed me to believe that you and I were on the same level.'

'As we are,' he insisted.

She laughed and shook her head. 'That's a fantasy. You're a prince and a billionaire, and who am I?'

'The most determined woman I've ever met.'

'Flattery doesn't wash with me, Luca. We had sex, the deepest intimacy of all, and then you simply turned your back and walked away. That means one thing to me. You're incapable of feeling.'

'You disappeared and pitched up here. Is that so different?'

'I was never going to stay in Italy for ever. It was a once-in-a-lifetime opportunity for me. I always knew I'd come home at some point. And now I intend to study and go on to make a purposeful life. You might be used to women throwing themselves at you, but—'

'Not in the way that just happened,' he said dryly.

She couldn't bear this. She couldn't bear the mash-up of feelings inside her. Her body was bruised. Her thoughts were in turmoil. She was in love with Luca. Their short, passionate time in Italy had left an indelible brand on her heart, but he was a man she could never have. He knew that as well as she did, surely?

'There's fault on both sides,' Luca insisted. 'You didn't reply to my letters. You refused to see me. You rejected my gifts. And, yes, I can see it must have seemed to you that I'd callously walked away, but I hope you can see now that there was a very good reason for my absence. Spend some time in Fabrizio. See the type of life our child will have.'

Fear speared through her at his words. *Hormones.* She knew she was overreacting, but he would sweep her away if she let him. He would expect the royal child to live with him. Yes, she should get to know his world. Luca was no ordinary man. She could never compete with his wealth, or royal status, but she believed just as strongly in her own values, and in her ability to bring up their child. They had to talk, but not right now. 'My cab's here—' She looked at his hand on her arm.

'What are you proposing, Callie?'

Luca's tone had changed, hardened. Their baby wouldn't benefit from parents at war. 'Truce,' she said. 'I'm proposing a truce. You're a hero. You saved me. You saved our child's life. I can never thank you enough for that. If nothing else, I'm sure we can be friends.'

'Friends?' Luca frowned.

'Please? For the sake of our child.'

Her cab rolled up at the kerb. Talking was done. He ground his jaw. Why wouldn't she take the lift he'd offered? He could call up a diplomatic limousine in minutes. Was this how it was going to be? He couldn't allow Callie a free hand. The heir to Fabrizio was too precious for that.

'I can't believe my new phone is still in one piece,' she said, glancing at it before putting it away.

'Give me your number.' He pulled out his phone.

'Give me *your* number,' she countered, 'and I'll call you when I'm ready.'

'Can I at least know where you're going,?'

'I'll call you,' she said as she climbed into the cab.

Seething inside, he gave her his number. After the accident and the shock of seeing him, he had to cut her some slack, but seeing Callie again was non-negotiable. He had every intention of keeping track of his unborn child. Grinding his jaw as the cab drove away, he had to remind himself this wasn't the end of anything, but just the start of their return match.

If her feelings had been mixed up before, they were ready to explode by the time she walked down the steps of the civic building to find Luca waiting outside. Lounging back against a sleek black car, he was staring at her with the lazy confidence that suggested he knew exactly what had happened at her job interview. *Of course he knew.*

Firming her jaw, she quickened her step towards him. The sooner they got this over with, the better. She'd had her suspicions at the start of her interview. It hadn't taken her long to realise she was never going to get the job, and the director of tourism was just curious to meet her. Even he'd admitted she was everything they were looking for; gregarious and well informed, she had read up on the history of the famous illuminations from the nineteenth century to the present day.

'And I know every nook and cranny of the town,' she'd assured him, explaining she'd visited Blackpool on numerous occasions.

'In short, you're perfect for the job,' he agreed, just before he shuffled awkwardly in his seat and explained that the vacancy was no longer available.

So why see her at all? Callie had wondered, until the director of tourism had added, 'Don't look so disappointed. I'm told you have a glittering future ahead of you.'

'What did it cost you?' she challenged Luca tensely. She'd come to a halt in front of him, and was determined to get the truth out of him, whatever it took.

'Cost me?' He frowned.

'How much did it cost you to spoil my chances for that job?' she demanded tight-lipped.

'Nothing,' he admitted.

'You're lying,' she said quietly.

'I think you should calm down,' Luca remarked as he opened the passenger door of his car. 'Climb in.'

'Not a chance.'

'Please.'

She started to walk past him, but he caught hold of her arm. 'Where do you think you're going?' he asked. 'You can't go back to the shop. It's all boarded up.' His voice was still low and even, but it had taken on an edge. 'Your landlady is spending the night in a very comfortable local hotel while my builders complete their repairs.'

'*Your* builders,' she snapped. 'That says it all. *Your* hand in my failure at interview just now. And you say you're not controlling? What else do you have in store for me, Luca?'

Releasing her arm, he stood back. 'I provided a faster solution for your landlady than her insurance company could hope to offer, and that is all. As for your job interview, how are you going to work as a tour guide when you're heavily pregnant? I can't risk the mother of my child being exposed to people who might exploit her to get at me. Your situation has changed, Callie, whether you like it or not.'

'It certainly has,' she agreed. 'I was free and now I'm not.' She was furious. 'How did you get an appointment to meet with the Director of Tourism so fast?'

'His secretary recognised me.'

'Of course she did. Since your enthronement you're all over the news. "The world's most eligible bachelor",' she quoted tensely, 'who just happens to have a pregnant and discarded mistress on the side.'

'Very dramatic,' he said.

'Dramatic? Since you came into my life, everything's been dramatic—' She bit off her angry words, remembering that without Luca she'd probably be dead and so would their unborn child. Hormones again, she realised. Definitely hormones. The next thing she knew there were tears in her eyes. She drove them back. 'You said it cost you nothing to stand in the way of me getting that job. What *did* you do, Luca? You must have said something?'

'I did,' he confirmed, shielding her as the wind blasted them. 'I offered reciprocal marketing of our two very different holiday destinations.'

'There must be more.'

'There was,' he confirmed evenly. 'I told him I wanted you to work for me.'

'What?'

'Get in the car.'

She was shivering violently. It was freezing cold. They stared at each other, unblinking. They both knew there could be no walking away this time. Callie had very little money left, and no-where to stay tonight. Even a simple boarding house at this time of year, when the illuminations were drawing crowds to the resort, cost far more than she could afford to spend.

'Where will you take me?' she asked.

'I thought you had a sense of adventure.'

'I don't like surprises.' But her options were zero. They had to speak at some point. Why not now? Surely two intelligent human beings could come to an amicable agreement?

Seriously?

Yes, because this wasn't about either of them, but about their child, and with their histories Callie was prepared to bet that both of them would put that child first.

The passenger door closed with a soft clunk, enclosing Callie in a very different world. This was a world that only the super-rich could afford. It wasn't the spicy warmth of the lemon groves, or the anodyne interior of a five-star hotel, but was so comfortable that it could easily muddle her mind. It was far too tempting to relax and not think of anything but getting to her destination, wherever that might be, safely and warmly. Soft classical music played in the background, while the scent of soft leather assailed her senses. In spite of all the warnings to self, she relaxed and drank it in.

This was the scent of money, she thought as Luca swung into the driver's seat. He only added to her pleasure with his natural warmth, and the scent of warm clean man, laced with the light, exotic fragrance he always wore. He pressed a button and the engine purred. The sexy black car pulled effortlessly out into the flowing traffic. There were no brash noises, no sharp edges, nothing to alarm. The vehicle was precision engineering at its finest, rather like the workings of Luca's mind.

He drove as smoothly and as skilfully as he did everything else. They were heading out of town, she noticed, towards the airport. She had some decisions to make, and had better make them fast. She had agreed to get in the car, but had she agreed to travel out of the country? The thought of seeing Luca on his home turf was an exciting prospect, but she was wary of being seduced into giving up her freedom. Even now she knew his true identity, he was still the most brutally handsome and desirable man. Her body ached and longed for him. Her mind told her they needed to talk. Her soul said they were meant to be together. On a far baser level, pregnancy had made her mad for sex, and there was only one answer to that.

CHAPTER EIGHT

THE ROYAL JET was waiting. On this occasion he would not be the pilot. He escorted Callie on board as if she were already his Princess. He understood her need for freedom. Theirs would be a marriage for practical reasons, tying neither of them down. Its sole purpose would be to provide Fabrizio with the longed-for heir. Would she agree to that proposal? Better this woman he cared for than some unknown princess from Michel's list, and it would fulfil Callie's wish for independence.

Callie would certainly agree to sex. Pheromones were threatening to drown him. Electricity wasn't just snapping, it was threatening to bring down the national grid. Taking her by the wrist, he led her straight to the rear of the plane where his private quarters were located. He had given instructions that they were not to be disturbed under any circumstances, short of an aviation meltdown. They didn't speak. They didn't need to. Callie's needs were flashing like neon signs. They'd talk later. Opening the door to his lavish suite, he ushered her inside.

'Luca—'

'Too much talking.' She was still wearing high heels and her prim interview suit. 'Keep the shoes on.'

'What?'

'You heard me. Take everything else off.' She had the best legs on earth, elongated by the high-heeled shoes, and a figure to die for. The height of the heels thrust her hips forward in a way he found irresistible. Caging her with his arms either side of her face, and his fists planted against the door, he brushed his lips against hers for the sheer pleasure of hearing her moan.

'All my clothes?' she asked, snatching a breath.

'Yes.'

Erotic heat clouded her eyes. 'You haven't told me where you're taking me.'

'You're going to love the surprise.'

'Let me decide,' she insisted. 'Tell me, then I'll take my clothes off.'

She was teasing *him*?

'You don't play fair,' she gasped as he pressed his body against hers.

'Have you only just noticed?'

Rolling his hips, he rubbed his body against her while she groaned. When he pulled back she moved frantically towards him in an attempt to repeat the contact. The jet engines whined into life right on cue. The aircraft was ready for take-off. Any time soon there would be the most enormous thrust and they'd take to the sky. 'You're overdressed,' he commented.

'Why couldn't we talk in Blackpool?' she asked, playing for time, he guessed.

'In a hotel, somewhere anonymous and clinical? Wouldn't you rather be here?'

She gasped as he found her. 'I can't.'

'I think you'll find you can.' He dropped a kiss on her shoulder.

'Who lives like this?' she said, staring past him at the designer-led living quarters on board his state-of-the-art jet.

'Stop trying to distract yourself and enjoy.'

'No. I can't. *I can't...*'

'You must. I insist.' Using his tongue to tease his way into her mouth, he deepened the kiss and pressed her back against the door. Every inch of her felt amazing. Had he really thought he knew how much he'd missed her, missed this? He didn't have a clue. Using his thigh to edge her legs apart, he finished what he'd started. She went quite still and then cried out repeatedly. It was some time before she quietened.

Her eyes remained closed, Her breathing remained hectic. He caressed her breasts while she recovered, teasing nipples that had tightened into prominent buds very lightly with his thumbnail. Gasping out his name, she rested her head against his chest as he stroked and teased her.

'I think we should take this to bed,' he said at last.

She gave him a teasing look.'Shouldn't we be strapped in?'

'If that's what you'd like?' he offered.

'You're bad,' she said as he took her to see the

specially designed bed belt. 'For the billionaire who has everything, I presume?'

'For the turbulence,' he confirmed.

'Do you expect much turbulence?'

'I expect a great deal of turbulence.'

'You're worse than I thought,' she said, laughing and relaxed now.

'Worse than you know.' Bringing her into his arms, he kissed her. When he let her go she searched his eyes in a way that touched him somewhere deep. Callie didn't see herself as he saw her. She was a refreshing change. Most women of his acquaintance were overly self-aware, while Callie was oblivious to how attractive she was.

'Why are you looking at me like that?' she asked him softly.

'I'm anticipating having sex with you.'

'That's convenient.'

'Is it?'

'Yes.' She bit back a smile. 'Because I'm doing the same.'

He moved over her. She writhed beneath him. She opened herself to him, inviting him to explore. 'Now,' she said with a kitten smile that made him hungrier than ever. She quivered with arousal beneath his hands as he teased her lips apart with his tongue. As he deepened the kiss she melted against him. He pressed her into the bed to rediscover the contours of her body. She was driving him crazy with lust. He was driving them both crazy, with delay. Lifting her on top of him, he caressed her buttocks, stroking them as she sighed and groaned, until finally he clasped them to position her. Reversing positions, he brought her under him.

'What about your clothes?' she asked.

He started to undress, but Callie was ahead of him. Ripping off his clothes, she wasn't satisfied until they were both completely naked. Taking hold of her shoulders, he held her away from him so he could give her a long, hard look. 'I've missed you,' he ground out.

'I've missed you too.' She was trembling with excitement and anticipation, asking him with her body to be held, to be kissed, and to be pleasured until she was exhausted. He had no intention of falling short in any way. Throwing her onto her back, he hooked her legs over his shoulders. He took a long, appreciative look, and then dipped his head and feasted while Callie groaned and bucked.

'The bed straps,' she gasped out.

'Are you asking to be restrained?'

'Sounds as if we're about to take off,' she warned, turning her head on the pillows to listen.

He shrugged as the whine of the engines turned into an imperative roar. 'I think you could be right,' he agreed dryly. 'I definitely think you should be held firmly and safely in place.' Securing her in a few deft moves, he returned to finish what he'd started.

She didn't last long. *'Aaaah...'* The cry of pleasure seemed torn from her soul. It escalated into a series of rhythmical, primal sounds deep in her throat. They tormented him. She tormented him. His was a seriously painful state.

'Ah...ah...' she gasped out repeatedly, bucking so furiously that even the straps and his hands had a battle to contain her. Once she was capable of speech, she instructed, 'I need you inside me now,' with her customary bluntness.

This coincided with the pilot applying full

thrust. Pinning Callie's hands above her head on the bank of soft cushions, he did the same. The sensation as the aircraft soared and they did too, was mind-numbing. Whatever he'd imagined about sex with Callie again was nothing compared to this. She was perfection. Her inner muscles gripped him with a vigour he could never have anticipated, and from there it was a wild, furious ride to satisfaction. By the time the jet had levelled out, Callie had enjoyed at least three noisy climaxes, and was ready for more. When she was done, he turned her on her side. 'Curl up and let me touch you. I want to watch.'

They were both blunt in bed when it came to what they liked. Callie didn't just agree to his proposition, she used colourful language to outline exactly what was expected of him. She lifted her thigh to tempt him even more, and angled her hips so he could see everything. He sank deep with a groan of contentment. 'More,' she insisted. 'More.'

He felt as if his climax started at his toes and then flooded his entire body. They were engaged in a very primitive act. He was claiming his mate.

She was claiming hers. Where this could lead he had no idea, and he wasn't in any condition to reason things through sensibly. 'I only have one complaint,' he said, bringing her on top of him when they were quiet again.

'A complaint?' she queried.

'You should always wear more clothes so there are more to take off.'

She relaxed and smiled, and, sighing with contentment, she added, 'Well, that's your Christmas present sorted out.'

Then she fell silent. He realised it was only a matter of days before Christmas. There had been so much going on he hadn't even realised. 'Hey,' he whispered, seeing Callie frown. 'We're definitely going to be together at Christmas.'

'Are we?' Her voice was matter of fact. Her stare was deep and long.

'Yes,' he confirmed, stroking her back to soothe her. 'You're not going to be spending Christmas in one room over a shop. I want you to see where I live.'

'I know where you live.'

'I mean Fabrizio.'

'It's still a palace.' She sighed as if picturing a world filled with art treasures, flunkeys and hushed decorum, when the truth was a modern palace that was more of a workplace. He had homes across the world where he enjoyed complete privacy, but since his enthronement the palace had become his main residence. He had an apartment there. The palace in Fabrizio was the engine of the dynasty, but his wing was elegant and private. The boy from the gutters had come a long way. 'Where I live overlooks a lake and gardens, and has every comfort a child could need,' he reassured Callie.

Better than one room over a shop, he could see her thinking. 'I'm sure it's lovely,' she agreed, tense now. Turning her back on him, she pulled up the covers and pretended to sleep. She did drift off eventually, while he lay at her side with his arms folded behind his head, checking his plan to make sure there'd be no hitches.

When she woke, she sat up and spotted the selection of outfits on a rail immediately. 'Where did they come from?'

'The cabin attendant wheeled them in.'

'While I was asleep? In your arms?'

'You were well covered up. I asked my private secretary to make sure there were some dresses and accessories on board for you, for when you disembark.'

'I've got my suit.'

He glanced at the creased skirt and jacket, still lying on the floor where she'd dropped them. 'Well, I have to say, this is another first.'

'What is?'

'A woman refusing to look at a rail of clothes.'

'Chauvinist.' Grabbing a sheet around her, she swung off the bed. 'I didn't say I wouldn't look at them, but I must insist on paying for whatever I choose.'

'I would expect nothing less of you,' he assured her, straight-faced.

'Are you mocking me?' she demanded.

'Maybe a little,' he admitted wryly.

For a few seconds as they stared at each other, he was stunned by how Callie made him feel. He had always guarded his emotions, but with Callie that wasn't possible. Even with the Prince, his late father, it had been very much a man-to-man

relationship. He'd never had any softening influ-
ences in his life. Women had always been accessories in the past, a deal that worked well both
ways, but Callie was different, special. Tousle-
haired and flushed from sleep, she was drowsy-
eyed with contentment, but still ready to take him
on if she felt it necessary. His groin tightened
at the thought. Unfortunately there wasn't time.
They'd be landing soon. 'I'm looking forward to
seeing which outfit you choose.'

She hummed and shot him a warning look.

That was all it took. He'd been inactive long
enough. Crossing the cabin, he yanked her close
to plant a hard, hot kiss on her tempting mouth.
'Surprise me,' he whispered.

'Don't I always?'

He kissed her again.

'What was that for?' she demanded.

'A down-payment on later.'

'I won't be bribed,' she warned.

He laughed as he left the cabin. They'd slept
together, made love together, and been happy together. Now they had a deal to make that both
they and Fabrizio could live with. He was sure

of Callie in so many ways. She was full of light and love and passion, and was honest and direct to a fault. That didn't mean he could predict how she would react to the idea of raising their child in Fabrizio, but for him that outcome was non-negotiable.

She chose a simple outfit of jeans, crisp white shirt and a smart navy-blue blazer, teamed with a pair of mid-heeled boots. She felt comfortable, confident, and happy—until she saw the royal chauffeur, standing by the side of the big royal limousine. The imposing black vehicle flying the crimson and gold flag of Fabrizio on its bonnet, above a shield that displayed Luca's royal house in images of a lion, a rearing black stallion and a mandolin, was a real punch between the eyes, reminding her that Luca was a royal prince with all the money, power, and influence he could ever wish for, while she couldn't even get a job.

The chauffeur stood proudly to attention as Luca appeared at the door of the aircraft. He ushered her ahead of him. She felt exposed. The blazer and jeans didn't seem enough somehow now that Luca had changed into a smart, dark linen suit with a pale blue open-necked shirt. If he'd looked stunning before, he looked like a prince now. Then, she thought, *Stand tall, you've got as much right as anyone else to fall down the steps of an aircraft.*

'Take my arm,' Luca directed, making sure she didn't have another accident.

'Are you sure?' she asked, thinking he would not want to be seen with her in a way that could compromise him.

'Of course, so long as you give it back,' he said.

Lifting a brow as he stared at her, Luca made her laugh.

Turned out, it wasn't so hard, this royal business. Luca's humour helped. She smiled. The chauffeur smiled back. He saluted as he opened the door of the fabulous royal limousine, and she thanked him when he saw her safely inside.

'That wasn't so bad, was it?' Luca demanded as the chauffeur closed the door, enclosing them in the heavy silence Callie was fast becoming used to in these luxury vehicles.

'Not bad at all,' she admitted. 'Why are you

doing that?' she asked when he lowered the privacy screen.

'Because I want you.'

Luca was as blunt as she was. Reaching across the wide expanse of soft cream kidskin, he dragged her onto his lap. 'You should have chosen a dress.'

'Luc—' She was about to protest, but he cut her off with a blistering kiss, and at the same time his hand found her. 'Oh, no,' she groaned, yielding to the inevitable as she opened her legs a little more. 'Oh, no?' he queried. 'Does that mean you want me to stop?'

'Don't you dare,' she whispered, rubbing her still-tender lips against his sharp black stubble. 'I wish I'd chosen a dress too.'

'I'm sure we can manage,' Luca said as his fingers worked deftly on the fastening at her waist. 'It's not as if we're stuck for space.'

'But do we have time?' she asked as he pulled off her jeans and she pulled off her jacket, this time remembering to fold it neatly.

'Enough time,' Luca ground out. 'Now your thong?' he suggested, settling back to watch.

'What about your clothes?'

'What about my clothes?' Lowering his zipper, he freed himself, proving he was more than adequately prepared. Reaching out, he brought her onto his lap. 'Straddle me,' he insisted, 'and make it slow.'

She felt deliciously exposed with her legs widely spread, and deliciously excited when Luca's hand found her. He was right about taking it slowly. She would never grow used to the size of him.

He felt so good. Linking her hands around his neck, she allowed him to guide her carefully down. He decided the pace, while she concentrated on sensation. She cried out with disappointment when his grip tightened on her buttocks, and he lifted her almost off him. Her cries of complaint brought a smile to his face, and he slowly lowered her again. Pressing down on her buttocks made sure that the contact between them was complete. And then he began to move. His hips thrust, sending him deep inside her, and he upped the tempo with each stroke until she could only bury her face in his jacket and wait for release. When it came it was incredible, and he knew just how to prolong it.

'Better now?' he asked quietly as she subsided into a series of soft, rhythmical sighs.

Callie lifted her head. 'Is there time for more?'

With a soft laugh against her mouth, Luca obliged.

CHAPTER NINE

FABRIZIO WAS BEAUTIFUL and quaint, with winding cobbled streets, and tree-filled parks at every turn. People waved and cheered when they saw the royal car, and Luca lowered the window when Callie was dressed again, so he could wave back. His timing, as always, was impeccable. She had caught her first sight of his fabulous palace when they were a few miles away. Surrounded by ancient city walls, the royal palace of Fabrizio sat atop a hill from where the defenders of old could see their enemies coming for miles around. It was the most beautiful building she had ever seen with a grandeur that even his *palazzo* in Amalfi couldn't match. Where that had been wedding-cake pretty, this was royal splendour cast in stone, wrought iron and stained glass. When the royal limousine drew up in front of a wide sweep of stone steps, Luca helped her out of the car and then left her in the care of his housekeeper and a maid, while he hurried off into the building.

Having crossed an exquisite hall, full of shields and swords and ancient portraits, Callie was taken up a sweeping staircase to the first level where she was shown into the most beautiful light and airy apartment. Knowing it would be hers for the duration of her stay was just incredible. The delicately decorated French furniture, the Aubusson rugs yielding softly underfoot, the twinkling glass and antique ornaments, the gilded mirrors—*what was she doing here?*

She thanked the stiffly formal housekeeper and the maid tasked with looking after her. Waiting until the door closed behind them, she headed for the unbelievably beautiful bathroom to take a shower in an enclosure big enough to house an entire rugby team. There was every conceivable type of potion, cream and bath foam, not in their original containers, but in the most exquisite cut glass jars and jugs. Lifting the fragile lid on one of these, she inhaled deeply. And sneezed. She was a little bit allergic to scent. But not to Luca's scent, Callie reflected wryly as she turned full circle to admire the pink-veined marble walls. What was he doing now? she wondered as she glanced at the internal telephone. She didn't want him to think her desperate. Let him call her, she decided. *Please.*

There was no such thing as the hot water running out at the palace. She basked in the luxury of heat and fragrant scent until she felt thoroughly clean, cosy, and fresh again. Then she donned a fluffy robe and wondered what to do about clothes. Pushing her feet into slippers she found ready in the bathroom, that matched the robe, she returned to the bedroom with its panelling and paintings, and floating silk voile, drifting romantically in front of the open window. She suddenly felt incredibly homesick and reached for her phone. What she needed was someone down to earth to confide in, someone she could trust to act as an honest sounding board. Ma Brown answered on the first ring.

'Ma...'

'Yes, dear?'

Ma Brown's concerned tone both bolstered Callie and provided a much-needed wake-up call. She had never been a moaner, and she wasn't about to start now that she was about to become a mother. 'I don't want you worrying about me,' she stressed, 'so I'm giving you an update.'

'Ooh, lovely,' Ma Brown enthused.

Callie could just picture her dear friend, pausing mid baking, or ironing, or dusting, or stirring a pot of something delicious on the stove, to hear what Callie knew she had to make into a Christmas fairy tale so that Ma Brown would smile and share it with the family, rather than fret about Callie over Christmas. 'I'm in Fabrizio,' she began.

'I knew it!' Ma Brown exclaimed. 'You're with the Prince.'

'Yes. But there's something else—'

'You're pregnant!' Ma Brown shrieked before Callie had chance to say a word.

'I had intended to break it to you gently—'

Ma Brown wasn't listening. 'Has he proposed yet?'

'No,' Callie admitted.

'Why ever not?' Ma Brown demanded good-humouredly. 'Do you need me to come out there and prompt him? I will, if you like. I can easily catch a flight.'

'No,' Callie said again, this time laughing. Ma Brown's voice had soared at least an octave. She probably didn't need a phone to be heard in Fabrizio. 'I promise I can deal with it.'

'Tell me about his country, then,' Ma Brown compromised, snatching a noisy breath as she attempted to calm down.

To a casual listener, their conversation might have seemed a little blasé under the circumstances, but Ma Brown could always imply more by her tone than she said in words. The simple phrase, tell me about Fabrizio, for instance, promised that the subject of Callie's pregnancy had not been forgotten, but merely put on the back burner for now. One thing was certain. Ma Brown would always be on Callie's side. Missing out the fact that she should have been planning her future, rather than scrambling over Luca, having sex in his jet and then in his car, Callie cut straight to the particulars. 'Everything in Fabrizio looks as if it has been polished to a flawless sheen. Think Monte Carlo with a touch of Dubai—'

'Oo-er,' Ma Brown exclaimed, breathless with excitement. 'Go on,' she prompted.

'Luca's palace looks like something out of a fairy tale. It's like Cinderella's castle with turrets and crenellations. There's even a drawbridge over the moat.'

'Imagine the staff needed to look after that,' Ma Brown breathed in awe.

'And everyone wears uniform,' Callie confirmed to add to the picture. 'Sentries stand guard wearing black velvet tunics braided with gold—'

'Goodness,' Ma Brown cut in. 'Isn't that all a bit intimidating?'

You have no idea, Callie thought, but what she actually said was, 'Poof! Not for you and me, Ma.'

'That's the spirit,' Ma Brown exulted. 'I've read about the palace and how fabulous it is. The countryside around it is supposed to be equally beautiful. Tell me about that now.'

Hmm. Difficult topic, Callie thought as the silence extended. 'I was so excited on the drive from the airport to the palace I didn't take much notice,' she admitted truthfully. 'I'll make sure to check it out next time and let you know.'

Ma Brown hummed thoughtfully. 'I've taken quite an interest in your Prince since he rode to your rescue.'

'He's not *my* Prince, Ma.'

Ignoring this, Ma Brown continued, 'The late Prince has ancestry stretching back to the mists of time.'

Unlike Luca's, which stretched back to the gutters of Rome. Or her own, Callie reflected, which extended to a row of small, back-to-back houses in the same neighbourly terrace as the Browns, which she wouldn't exchange for the world. She couldn't imagine how she'd have got on when she was younger without the wonderful support of the family next door.

'When are you coming home, our Callie?'

'I'm not sure,' Callie admitted.

'If I were you, I'd stay there as long as you can,' Ma Brown cheerfully recommended. 'There's a grand ball soon in Fabrizio to celebrate Prince

Luca's enthronement. You can't miss that. I want to hear all about it.'

'I doubt I'll be invited,' Callie confessed. Luca hadn't mentioned a ball. She couldn't imagine he'd want her there. Thank goodness. Her stomach flipped at the thought of attending such a grand occasion, and then flipped at the thought of Luca attending the ball with an eager princess on his arm. He was better off with someone like that, she told herself, someone who was used to public occasions. Callie would probably say the wrong thing, or trip over her own feet.

'Don't let me down,' Ma Brown warned. 'When you said you were going on an adventure, a ball at the Prince's palace was exactly the sort of thing I had in mind.'

'I'm not Cinderella,' Callie reminded her good friend ruefully, 'and I don't have a fairy godmother.'

'I wouldn't be too sure about that,' Ma Brown insisted. '*And* I want an invitation to the wedding.'

Before Callie had chance to respond, Ma Brown

had bustled off the line, no doubt to attend to more motherly duties.

A diet of romance, Ma Brown's favourite reading matter, had obviously distanced her from reality, Callie concluded, but she was both thrilled and relieved at the way her good friend had taken the news of the pregnancy. Ma Brown was right. Pregnancy was normal. Attending a royal ball was not. But she'd have a go, if she were invited. She owed it to Ma Brown to attend the ball if she got the chance.

Ten minutes later she changed her mind again. *I don't belong here.* Burying her head in her arms, Callie took a deep, steadying breath, and then lifted her chin to stare at herself in the ornately gilded dressing-table mirror. Her reflection appeared in what was surely a priceless antique like everything else in her elegant suite of rooms. How on earth had she ended up here?

'I'll tell you how,' Callie's snarky inner critic butted in. 'From good girl to a hussy in no time flat, that's you, Callie Smith!'

Fair play, Callie agreed. The fairy tale wasn't quite as she'd described it to Ma Brown. She never knew where she stood with Luca, and the worst of it was, a few months ago, she'd known exactly where she was heading. Her short adventure in Italy would be a harmless interlude to look back on with pleasure. She'd go home after a couple of weeks, pick up her studies, go to college, and get a better job. Pregnancy had changed all that. Her priorities had completely switched around. The baby came first. It always would. Every decision Callie made from now on would be in the best interests of her child.

Luca's child also.

Closing her eyes, she reviewed what she'd seen of Luca's life to date. From the vast, echoing hallway, with it frescoes on the lofty ceiling, to the foot of a wide sweep of crimson-carpeted stairs, her head hadn't stop whirring as she gazed around. Did she need more proof that she didn't belong here? It hardly seemed possible that just a few hours ago she had been planning to make do and mend to raise a child she already loved. In the palace she was surrounded by so much… *everything*. The five-star hotel she'd thought so lavish was a mere potting shed compared to this.

She had to stop short of pinching herself to make sure it wasn't all a dream. When a knock came at the door and it opened without Callie saying a word, she sprang up guiltily.

'Oh, sorry, madam, I—'

'No—please, come in. And please call me Callie...'

Callie paled as the maid stood back against the wall to allow a team of footmen to wheel several gown rails into the room. These were laden with a sparkling array of full-length ball gowns. Cinderella had nothing on this, Callie concluded, frowning. 'There must be some mistake,' she said.

'No mistake, madam,' the maid assured her. 'As it's rather short notice, His Serene Highness apologises for not sending you an invitation to the ball, but he wants you to know that you are free to choose any of these dresses to wear.'

'His Serene Highness expects me to attend the ball?'

'He does, madam.'

Then, His Serene High and Mightiness could have the courtesy to come and tell her that himself, Callie thought, but she thanked the maid, who was the innocent messenger. 'I hope this hasn't put you to too much trouble?'

'None at all, madam. As soon as you've made your choice, if you ring this bell…' the maid indicated a silken tassel hanging on the wall '… I'll return immediately to help you dress.'

'The ball's tonight?' Callie exclaimed in panic.

'Oh, no, madam. This is just to give you chance to choose your gown and try it on. The Prince has instructed me to tell you that he will be with you by seven o'clock this evening to discuss your choice of gown.'

Hmm, Callie thought. And take it off, if she knew Luca. She couldn't imagine he cared less what she wore. He was far more interested in removing her clothes.

As soon as the maid had gone, she walked over to the rail to check out the selection of dresses. She'd never seen so many fabulous outfits before. There were gowns in every colour in the rainbow. Some were beaded, some had frills, and some had gauzy ribbon. Nearly all of them had low necks, and/or big slits up the side and plunging backs. She guessed she was ungrateful for thinking all of them a bit over the top. She was frightened to touch them in case she soiled them, but she had to choose one. Picking out an aquamarine gown, her favourite colour, she held it up against her, but it was so heavily beaded it weighed a ton. She had to admit that the scent of fine silk, and the sight of such expert tailoring, did take her breath. There was boning inside the bodice, so no need to wear a bra, and the skirt was such a slender column, she'd have to hop, Callie reflected wryly as she returned it to the rail.

One after the other she discarded the dresses. She couldn't see herself wearing any of them. They were far too fancy, and didn't look at all comfortable to wear. Crossing the room, she rang the bell.

'Yes, madam?' the maid enquired politely.

'We're around the same size. Could you lend me a pair of jeans and a top so I can go shopping?' There must be a high street in Fabrizio, she reasoned.

'Go *shopping*, madam?' the maid repeated as if

Callie had suggested dancing naked in the street. 'I'll have a selection of outfits delivered to you within the hour.'

'Really?'

'Of course.'

'Okay, but be sure to give me the—' Before she had chance to say, 'receipt, so I can pay the bill,' the maid had left the room and closed the door.

Callie heaved a sigh. What was she supposed to do now? She tried to ring Luca, but that was like trying to get hold of the Queen of England. She went through half a dozen people and none of them would put her through to him. It was already nine o'clock in the evening. He'd left her alone to stew. Talking of which, she was hungry. Picking up the internal phone, she rang the kitchen to order a tray of sandwiches and a pot of tea. Hmm. So much for the high life! And so much for the discussions they were supposed to be having. Could matters of State be so much more important than their child?

She drank the tea, ate the sandwiches, then walked around the apartment until she knew every inch of it by heart. It was a gilded cage for

the Prince's pet bird, Callie concluded. It was im-
personal. The drawers were empty. There wasn't
even a book to be found. There certainly wasn't
anything as crass as a TV. Opening the glass
doors onto her private veranda, she sat down at
the wrought-iron table. Listening to the night
sounds soothed her. It was a beautiful evening,
but where was Luca? She should have known by
now that sex meant nothing to him, and he could
just walk away, forget it, forget her.

She went back into the room when it began
to get chilly. She'd forgotten that the maid had
promised to have more clothes delivered, and the
room was full of them. She couldn't deny that
rooting through the boxes and carrier bags was
fun. Choosing a pair of jeans and a loose sports
top, she exchanged her fluffy robe for a casual
look that would take her through to bedtime.

More tea?

More tea.

She was just concluding, with a return of good
humour, that wading through such a vast selection of clothes was exhausting, when the door
opened and Luca walked in.

'Tea, madam?'

She almost jumped out of her skin. Even with a tray of tea in his hands, he was everything she could desire in a man. Dark, tall, and powerfully built. She would never get used to the breath-stealing sight of him. He'd changed into jeans and a crisp white shirt with the sleeves rolled up. *Those arms!* His jeans were cinched with a heavy-duty belt that drew attention to his washboard waist. His shoulders were epic and his powerful forearms were tanned and shaded with just the right amount of dark hair.

Those arms belonged around her, she concluded, forgetting her good intentions as he strode across the room. She was supposed to be having a serious discussion with him, not falling victim to his dazzling charm. *Be objective*, she told herself firmly.

'Ah, the dresses have arrived,' he commented as his stare swept over the gown rail. 'Now for the fashion show.' Throwing himself down on a finely upholstered chaise longue, he made a gesture she could only presume was supposed to goad her into action.

'Are you going to model them for me, then?' she asked. 'You mentioned a fashion show?' she prompted when Luca raised a brow.

For a moment he looked bemused and then he laughed. 'You never change, do you?'

'I hope not. Hooking up in a car does not a future make, Prince Luca. You and I have some serious talking to do.'

'Soon,' he promised. 'But first a toast,' he insisted, standing up.

'In tea?' she queried.

'I can send for champagne—'

'I can't—'

'Of course you can't.' With a grimace, he reached for her, and, jerking her close, he linked their fingers in a way she found very hard to resist. 'Forgive me,' he whispered, slanting a grin. 'I had forgotten why we're here for the moment.'

'Don't,' she warned with a straight look into his eyes.

'I was about to propose a toast to the heir to the principality of Fabrizio,' he explained.

She hummed. 'In that case, I'll forgive you.'

When Luca smiled his wicked smile, if it hadn't

been for the sexual tension between them they were close enough in that moment to be just two friends enjoying a moment of trust between themselves.

'Have you chosen your ball gown yet?' he asked, turning to glance at the packed gown rail.

'I want you to feel comfortable. I know you'll look beautiful. It's going to be a special night for both of us, because this is my chance to introduce you to my guests.'

'As what?' she asked.

Luca appeared to ponder this. 'My personal assistant? No.' His lips pressed down as he shook his head. 'What about Keeper of the Crown Jewels? More accurate?'

'This is serious,' Callie warned. 'Please stop teasing me. If I'm going to attend my first ball with you, I need to know where I stand. That's the only way I'm going to feel comfortable.'

'Comfortable was the wrong word. I can see that now,' Luca admitted. 'I want you to feel sensational. As the ball is tomorrow evening you'd better choose one of these gowns to make sure you do.'

But that wasn't what she was here for. She had come to Fabrizio to talk about their baby.

What about the promise she'd made to Ma Brown to send a full report on the ball? Callie glanced at the glamorous gowns twinkling on the rail. She wouldn't be able to get into any of them in a few months' time, not that she'd have any use for a ball gown when she went home. 'I'll look ridiculous,' she fretted as she rifled through the rail.

'You'll look beautiful,' Luca argued, making himself comfortable. 'Let's make a start.'

'I'll change in the dressing room,' she said, picking out the aquamarine gown that had first caught her eye. 'And I'm not coming out if I look a freak.'

Safe behind the door to her dressing room, Callie stared at herself in the mirror and grimaced. The gown that had looked so pretty on the rail did fit well, but, apart from being so heavy, it was too tight. It pushed her breasts up and her confidence down. But that wasn't what really worried her. When she emerged from the dressing room,

Luca agreed. 'You look like a mermaid,' he said as she wiggled her way across the room.

'Thank goodness that's a no.'

'Unless you plan to hop into position at my side?' he suggested.

'I could drift towards you in this,' she suggested when she had changed into the next dress, a coral number with long chiffon floats flying from each shoulder.

'Nah. You'll only get caught in the door.'

'You know me too well.'

'I'm getting there,' Luca admitted dryly as Callie chose another dress.

'This one?' she asked uncertainly, blowing fronds of fern-like decoration away from her face.

'You look like a market garden,' Luca dismissed as she performed a twirl.

True enough, the big floral pattern wasn't her best look.

'What about this one?' he suggested, selecting a plain, intricately beaded flesh-coloured gown.

'Yes. That's nice,' she agreed. 'I'll try it on.'

With the dressing-room door closed between

them again, Callie stared at her reflection in amazement. She actually looked quite good. Smoothing the delicate fabric over her frame, she had to admit that the gown Luca had chosen was both elegant and sexy. She might have known he'd have exquisite taste. The shade of the fabric matched her skin tone so exactly it was almost possible to imagine she was naked. Naked and shimmering with a slit up the side of the dress that almost reached her waist. Taking a deep breath, she opened the door.

Luca said nothing at all. His face was completely expressionless. This was Luca at his most dangerous, she thought. 'No,' she warned when he stood up and prowled towards her.

'Why not?' he husked. 'It's not as if I can make you pregnant.'

'Luca!'

He swallowed her protests in a kiss, and it wasn't just a kiss but a whole-body experience that made her hunger for him eclipse everything. His hands were warm on her body. He knew every slope and curve. The gown was so sheer, so delicate, that his touch transmitted effortlessly through it as if they were both naked. Memories bombarded her, memories of pleasure, memories of trust.

'I want you,' he growled. 'Right here. Right now. I can't wait.'

'Neither can I,' she assured him fiercely.

Luca had already found the slit at the side of the dress. She only had to move slightly for his fingers to brush dangerously close to where she needed him. Her breath caught as he handled her with the skill that promised so much more. She was wearing nothing beneath the gown but a flimsy thong. Held together with not much more than a hope and a prayer, the thong stood no chance against Luca's assault. Ripping it off, he cast it aside and rammed her up against the wall. Breath shot out of her as his hand found her. With teasing strokes, he tested her readiness. That didn't take long. Freeing himself, he nudged his thigh between her legs and, dipping at the knees, he took her in one long, firm thrust. From there it was a wild, noisy ride to their goal, but even when she shrieked as she lost control he kept on plunging until her throat was hoarse, and her body was alight with pleasure.

'I can't feel you,' she complained when she was able to talk again.

'What?' Luca demanded, frowning into her eyes.

'Not that—' She groaned with pleasure as he flexed inside her. 'I mean your naked body,' she explained. Tugging at his shirt, she made her meaning clear. 'I want to feel all of you hot and hard against me.' They ripped his clothes off between them and tossed them aside. 'Better!' she approved as his heat rasped against her body.

'Still not enough for you,' he guessed. Taking hold of her hands, he pinned them above her head, and with his other hand locked around the front of her dress, he ripped it from her body.

The beautiful gown was shredded, ruined. Disaster. But she didn't care. All that mattered was this. Rubbing her breasts against him tormented her nipples until they were taut little buds, composed entirely of sensation. They had a direct link to her core, and her hips worked involuntarily in her desperation for more contact. She couldn't remain still. She couldn't remain quiet. She was noisy and demanding. Scrambling up him, she locked her legs around his waist.

'More?' he suggested in the deep, gravelly voice with its flavour of Italy that could always make her tingle.

'Are you purposely withholding pleasure from me?' she demanded.

Luca laughed softly. 'As if I'd dare.'

'Don't make me wait,' she warned.

His answer was to nuzzle her neck with his sharp black stubble until she was a seething mass of lust. 'I just asked, did you want more?' he reminded her.

He surely didn't expect an answer to that question.

CHAPTER TEN

THE BALL GOWN was ruined. No point worrying about that now. She'd skip the ball. That was the last thought in Callie's head as Luca made rational thought impossible. He was making love to her. This wasn't just sex. They were natural together. This was so good, so right. This was fierce. When the moment came, she was wild with fear of the precipice she was facing, but Luca husked soothing words of reassurance and encouragement in his own language as he kissed her over the edge.

'Greedy,' he whispered when she quietened.

'You make me greedy,' she complained, smiling with contentment as she crashed against his chest.

Finding the nook just below his shoulder blade, she snuggled close as he carried her to the bed.

A deep sense of this being right filled her completely. They belonged together. He laid her down gently on the bed and came to lie with her. When he brought her into his arms, her breathing slowed and her limbs grew weightless. Problems nagged at the back of her mind, but they could wait until tomorrow. Right now she could do nothing more than close her eyes and drift away.

He held Callie in his arms all night, watching her sleep. As he did so, he went over what lay ahead of her. It wouldn't be an easy transition for her from the freedom of a normal life to all the restrictions of royalty, but if anyone could cope, she could. And he'd be with her every step of the way. He was confident that Callie would adapt to royal life as quickly as he had. He'd rebelled at first, but then he'd been very young. Callie was clever and kind, and her sense of humour would ease her through the sticky patches. Her common sense would get her through the rest. Not only would he have the longed-for heir, but a new, fresh style of Princess who would care for the land he had come to love as deeply as he did.

Careful not to wake her, he left Callie at dawn.

Breakfast meetings were the norm for him. With her hair tousled, and her face still flushed with sleep, she had never looked more desirable, but he was a slave to duty. Both his royal council and his business concerns called him this morning. And then there was the ball tonight. He grimaced as he glanced at the gown he'd ruined. But there were plenty more on the rail. Callie would have to forget about being understated for one night, and just choose one of them.

Callie woke slowly, cautiously. At first she didn't know where she was. Her head was ploughed into a stack of pillows scented with lavender and sunshine. The bed was firmer than she was used to, the duvet softer…and her body felt very well used. With a groan of contentment, she turned her face, relishing the touch of the smooth white cotton, and inhaled deeply. Slowly, it all came back to her. Reaching out a hand, she searched for Luca, and stilled when she discovered the bed at her side was empty. Sitting up, she could see the indentation of his head on the pillow, so she hadn't imagined last night. She really was at the palace. *The palace!* In the most sumptuous suite of rooms imaginable. *Incredible.* But it was very quiet. She stilled and knew at once she was alone.

Hearing a knock on the door, she hastily pulled up the sheet to cover her naked body. 'Yes?' It had to be the maid. Spotting what remained of the glamorous gown still strewn on the floor, she called out, 'Just a minute,' and leapt out of bed. Gossip would spread like wildfire in the palace. Why fan the flames? Gathering up the dress, she brought it back to the bed, and stuffed it out of sight beneath the bedding. 'Come in,' she called out brightly.

The maid entered carrying a breakfast tray. There was a single red rose in a silver vase on the tray. 'From His Serene Highness,' the maid explained as she set down the tray. 'He has suggested that you rest this morning in preparation for the ball.'

Recover, he meant, Callie thought dryly, showing nothing of her thoughts on the passionate night before on her face. 'Thank you for bringing my breakfast,' she said warmly, 'but I will be getting up.'

'Oh, and this arrived by courier,' the maid said as she handed Callie a package she had lodged under her arm.

'For me?' Callie exclaimed with surprise.

She bolted breakfast as the maid opened the curtains and threw the windows wide. She couldn't wait to open the unexpected parcel, but wanted to do so when she was alone.

'Anything else I can get for you?' the maid asked politely before she left.

'Nothing. Thank you.'

Turning over the large padded envelope, Callie smiled broadly. The bold handwriting gave the game away, as did the UK stamp. 'Ma Brown,' she breathed. 'What have you done now?'

What Ma had done was to go shopping at a popular high street store, where she'd found the perfect dress for Callie to wear at the ball. Callie gasped with pleasure as she held it up and saw her reflection. The dress was simple and elegant. At last, a dress she could feel comfortable in. She'd take a shower and then she'd try it on.

The fine flesh-coloured fabric slithered over Callie's naked body like a second skin. It couldn't have fitted her better. The design was uncannily similar to the gown that lay ruined on the bed. The popular brand was a known fast follower that could have catwalk looks available for sale within hours. She would go to the ball, Callie concluded with amusement as she slipped on a pair of high-heeled shoes, and in a dress worth infinitely more to her than all those expensive gowns on the rail put together. Picking up her phone to thank her best of friends, she smiled with pleasure. 'Oh, Ma Brown, you've really come up trumps this time,' she murmured as she waited for the call to connect.

It was the evening of the grand ball and all his guests had arrived, but where was Callie? He wasn't accustomed to waiting. Tonight of all nights, a late arrival was unacceptable. Her maid had been given strict instructions regarding timing. Royals were expected to be punctual. Everything ran to clockwork precision. There was no leeway for a few minutes either way. With impatience, he turned his attention from the entrance where Callie was due to appear, to the guests who were waiting to meet him.

Laughter and excitement filled the room. There was a huge sense of expectation. No one had refused his invitation to the ball. There were rumours of an announcement tonight and interest was running high. He felt a great sense of love and gratitude for the restoration his father, the late Prince, had carried out so efficiently on the glorious old building, and this did soothe him to some small degree. The ballroom was a glittering spectacle with huge chandeliers glittering like diamond globes beneath a domed sky of priceless frescoes. An orchestra of the most talented Viennese musicians set the mood. Waiters in black dress trousers and short white jackets, braided with the royal colours, carried solid gold trays bearing a selection of canapés prepared by the world's top chefs. There were two champagne fountains, as well as tall crystal flutes of vintage champagne being offered to guests at priceless French ormolu tables that lined the room. Nearly every country was represented. Splendidly dressed royals dripping in family jewels mingled with diplomats and top-ranking soldiers. No one was too proud to sup at his table. Guessing that tonight would be talked about for years had winkled out even the most standoffish royal. Everyone was keen to see how the boy from the gutters had transformed into a prince.

So where was she?

There was no excuse for this. He had instructed his private secretary to commission the finest hairdressers and beauticians to assist Callie with her preparations for tonight. He couldn't believe her personal maid had failed to get her out on time. Did Callie hope to slip in unnoticed? Was she coming at all?

He gave a grim shrug. Callie Smith was the one woman he could never predict. Summoning a footman, he sent a message to Signorina Smith's maid to ask how much longer she would be. The man hurried off, leaving Luca to seethe in silence.

Well, this was it, Callie concluded as two liveried footmen swung the gilded double doors wide. She had politely asked the hairdressers and make-up artists to leave, preferring to get ready by herself, and now there was just this small hurdle of a ballroom packed with the great and good to overcome. She inhaled sharply at the scene of dazzling glamour, and was almost blinded by the flash of diamonds and the light flaring from countless chandeliers. *Trust me to forget my tiara tonight*, she mused wryly. Lifting her chin, she walked forward.

'Signorina Callista Smith.'

Callie glanced around as the disembodied voice of a famous television personality announced her arrival at the ball.

'That's you, miss,' one of the friendly footmen who'd opened the door for her prompted in an exaggerated stage whisper.

'Thank you,' she whispered back.

In the time it had taken Callie to say this, every head had turned her way. Even the orchestra paused, leaving her at the top of a dizzying flight of marble steps. The solid mass of people below her looked impenetrable, and not exactly welcoming. Her throat dried. She clenched her hands into fists at her side. She could only pray the stiletto heels fairy was on her side tonight.

'Wait...'

Every head swivelled to stare at Luca. His familiar voice stripped the tension from her shoulders. Her gaze fixed on him as the crowd parted to let him through. Whatever remained of her breath flew from her lungs as he strode forward. In full dress uniform, with his sash of office drawing attention to his powerful chest, this was the man she remembered, the man her body rejoiced in, the man she laughed with, slept with, and enjoyed challenging, as Luca relished tormenting her, and right now he looked good enough to eat.

'May I?' he asked, offering his arm as he prepared to lead her down the stairs.

'Thank you.' She smiled—graciously, she hoped.

If a pin *had* dropped, it would most certainly have deafened her. It appeared that no one breathed, let alone spoke, as Luca steered her safely down the steps.

'You look beautiful,' he whispered.

'I'm sorry I took so long,' she whispered back. 'The hairdresser made me look like a freak, so I had to redo everything. And don't even ask about the make-up.'

'But you aren't wearing any.'

'Exactly,' she murmured. 'If you'd seen me with false eyelashes and red-apple cheeks you'd have run a mile.'

'Would I?' he murmured, sounding unconvinced.

They'd reached the dance floor by this time. Everyone was staring, but just being with Luca reassured her, and she didn't hesitate when he asked her to dance.

Callie came into his arms like a rather lovely boat floating effortlessly into its mooring. The intimacy between them must have been obvious to everyone, and the shocked silence that had first greeted her changed at once to a buzz of interest.

'I can just imagine what they're saying,' she breathed.

'Do you care?' he replied.

'No,' she assured him. 'I just wish I was barefoot. You're in serious danger of being stabbed.'

'Not a chance,' he whispered.

He laughed. She relaxed, and the glamorous ball continued.

'Where did you get the beautiful dress?' he asked. 'You look stunning. It's so elegant. I didn't see it on the rail. It's so delightfully simple, compared to other women's more elaborate gowns.'

'That's the secret of its allure,' she assured him with a cheeky smile. 'Ma Brown,' she whispered discreetly.

'Well, wherever it came from, you couldn't look lovelier.'

'Well, thank you, kind sir…you don't look too bad yourself.'

She was in his arms, and, as far as he was concerned, that was all that mattered. 'Do you find it warm?' he asked.

'Is this another of your euphemisms, which could be interpreted as let's find a tree?'

'Callie Smith,' he scolded softly with his mouth very close to her ear.

'You left me alone, abandoned me, and now you can't get enough of me?'

'Correct.'

'Don't you have any scruples?'

'Hardly any,' he confessed. 'I'm planning to take you to see a magical gazebo.'

'Filled with your etchings?' she guessed.

He laughed, and was further amused by the fact that people dancing close to them were hanging on their every word. Leading Callie off the dance floor, he led her through towering glass doors onto a veranda stretching the entire length of the palace. Even this late in the year, plants illumi-nated by blazing torches still flowered profusely, and their fragrance filled the air. He wouldn't usually notice such things, but being with Cal-lie always heightened his senses. A pathway led through the formal lawn gardens, and where they ended there was a lake with an island at its heart. Lights glinted on the island, and a rowing boat was moored alongside the small wooden pier that stretched out into the lake.

'Really?' Callie queried with a pointed glance at her dress and shoes.

'Where's your sense of adventure?' he de-manded.

Slipping off her shoes, she accepted his steadying hand as she gingerly boarded the boat. 'I used to escape the palace by rowing out to the island,' he explained when he joined her. He'd left his uniform jacket and white bow tie on the shore with his highly polished shoes. Freeing a few buttons at the neck of his shirt, he sat across from her and reached for the oars.

'I can understand why you might want to be alone here,' Callie agreed as she trailed her fingertips in the water. 'It's so beautiful and peaceful on the lake.'

'I didn't notice that when I was a youth,' he admitted, plunging the oars into the mirror-smooth water. 'It took time for me to trust the Prince, my father, and sometimes I was just angry for no reason and just wanted to get away. Now I think I was afraid of disappointing him. I'd only known rare acts of kindness on the streets, and the fact that he never gave up on me seemed to be just one more reason for me to put him to the test.'

'That's only natural.'

'I was lucky.' He put his back into the stroke and as he saw Callie's appreciative gaze focus on his bunching muscles his impatience to reach the opposite shore grew.

'How did you live,' she asked, 'back before the Prince found you?'

He shrugged and dipped the oars again. 'I cleaned around the market stalls in return for spoiled fruit, stale bread, and mouldy cheese. I had some good feeds,' he remembered, 'but the stallholders had many calls on their time, and I was proud even then. I might have been filthy and wearing rags but I vowed that I would never sink any lower and would always strive to rise. My bathroom was the Tiber, and my bedroom better than most people could boast.'

'What do you mean by that?' she asked.

'I slept at the Coliseum,' he explained. 'I came to know a member of the security staff, and he turned a blind eye when I curled up in the shadows of that great arena.'

'You make it sound romantic,' Callie said with a frown, 'but you must have been freezing in winter.'

'It was certainly a challenge,' he recalled, 'but atmospheric too. I used to sleep in Caesar's box, rather than in the dungeons where the poor victims used to languish as they awaited their terrible fate. I had nothing in the material sense,' he added as their small craft sliced through the water, 'except when it came to determination. I had plenty of that, as well as the freedom to change my condition, which I did.'

'What age were you when this was happening?'

'I was grubbing around the streets from the age of four. That was when my mother died,' he explained. 'The whorehouse where she worked kicked me out. In fairness, no one could spare the time to take care of me. I think now that I was better off by myself. The clientele at the brothel weren't too choosy who they abused, if you take my meaning.'

'I do. But how did you manage on your own on the streets at the age of four?'

'There were other, older children on the streets. They showed me how to stay alive.'

'How did you end up at the Coliseum?'

'A lot of homeless children slept there. I saw the tourist posters advertising this colossal building, and I wanted to see it for myself. Getting inside was easy. I just joined the queue of tourists and walked straight in. I soon learned that if I pretended to be a lost child, concerned attendants would feed me. It worked for quite a while until they began to recognise me, but by then they had developed a soft spot for the boy from the gutters and so they turned a blind eye. The people who worked at the Coliseum didn't have much money, either, and so they saved food from the trash for me to root through. There were plenty of half-eaten burgers and hot dogs for supper. I don't remember being hungry. The Coliseum was like a hotel for me, growing up, so don't feel sorry for me. I did fine. The Coliseum was both my home and my school. I saw everything you can imagine during my time there. I learned about sex, violence, thieving, unkindness, and great acts of kindness too.'

'Can you remember your parents?' she asked as he took a deep pull on the oars.

'Nothing I care to bring to mind,' he admitted dryly. 'My mother was always harassed and often sick. I think now that she was what we would call depressed. No surprise there, but a child can't understand why a person behaves the way they do. A child only knows that it's hungry, or frightened, and I knew I had to fend for myself long before she died.'

'And your father? Did you ever meet him?'

'He turned up one night,' Luca recollected. He huffed a short, humourless laugh. 'My mother's colleagues pelted him with rotten fruit and worse. I remember him standing on the street, shouting up at her open window. I remember his angry voice, and his soiled white shirt and the glint of his gold earrings.'

'He doesn't sound very nice.'

He shrugged. 'Who knows?'

'And now you're a prince with a country to rule and a palace to live in. It must all seem quite incredible, even now?'

'No. It seems right,' he said thoughtfully. 'If there was luck involved, it was that I met the Prince, the best of men, and a man who changed my life. Though even that wasn't as simple as it sounds,' he admitted. 'After everything I'd seen, I wasn't easily impressed—not even by the Prince of Fabrizio.'

'How did he persuade you to leave the streets and come to live with him?'

'He was a patient man,' Luca said, thinking back. 'From the moment he found me stealing food from the bins and the buffet table during his royal visit to the Coliseum, he was determined to save me. He told me this years later.'

'What did he do about your stealing?' Callie asked as he shipped the oars.

'He asked his attendant to find me a shopping bag, so I didn't have to hide my hoard down my shirt.'

'Cool,' she said, smiling.

'Oh, he was that,' he agreed as he sprang onto the shore to moor up.

She placed her hands in his as he helped her onto the dock. He wanted to take her right there. Throw her down on the cool wood and make love to her until she didn't have the strength to stand, but delay was its own reward.

It was just a small island. She could probably walk around it in ten minutes, Callie thought. The grass was cool and green, and felt lush and thick beneath her naked feet. Picking up the hem of her dress, she stared around. The clustering trees were lit with thousands of tiny lights in celebration of the ball. And then she saw the gazebo he'd talked about ahead of them. 'Is this where you used to come and sulk?' she asked.

'How did you guess?'

As he swung around to face her, the pulsing heat of desire surged through her. 'I've been a teenager too.'

He laughed and held out his hands. She felt so safe and warm when he took hold of her, and Luca's kisses were always a drugging seduction. They seemed even more so here on this magical island. Just occasionally, fairy tales did come true. She wanted to believe it so badly as he kissed her again. She'd spent so much of her life bottling up emotion, but Luca knew how to set it free, and as his kisses grew more heated she knew she would take any and every chance to hold onto happiness.

He swung her off her feet and strode quickly to the entrance to the gazebo. Lowering her down, he steadied her and then pressed her back against the wooden structure. Caging her with his arms either side of her face, he brushed his lips against her mouth and smiled. It was the most romantic moment, but if she'd written the fairy tale herself she could never have predicted what he'd say next. 'Marry me, Callie. Marry me and become my Princess.'

At first she thought she was imagining it, and it was all a dream, until Luca repeated softly, 'Marry me, Callie.'

She stared into his eyes, struggling to compute what he'd said. Embarrassed, uncertain, she resorted to teasing him. 'Shouldn't you be down on your knees? Or, one of them, at least?'

'I need an answer,' Luca said, refusing to respond to her lighter tone. 'Just a straight yes or no will do. Or are you playing for time?'

'No,' she argued. 'I'm playing for the highest of stakes of all. I'm playing for my heart, and for the future of our child.'

'Then, marriage makes perfect sense,' he insisted.

'Does it?' She frowned.

'You know it does.'

Smiling into her eyes, he kissed her again, and because she wanted him she was foolish enough to believe in the fairy tale for now.

CHAPTER ELEVEN

'TRUST ME,' LUCA said as he took her slow and deep. They had been making love on the soft cushions in the gazebo for what felt like hours. 'Trust me,' he said again as he soothed her down.

'Shouldn't you get back to the ball?' she asked. She was snuggled up tightly against Luca, whose protective arms wrapped securely around her.

'If you're ready, we'll go back,' he murmured as he planted a kiss on the top of her head.

'Bathe in the lake first?' she suggested.

They swam, then dried off together, and Callie dressed quickly, thanking her lucky stars she had short hair that didn't take long to dry in the warm night air. Slipping her simple dress on, she took hold of Luca's hand and they walked back to the boat; back to reality, she thought, but if he could carry this off—their absence would have been noted—then so could she.

'My lords, ladies and gentlemen, I have an announcement to make...'

Silence fell the instant Luca's deep and distinctive voice was heard through the hidden speakers in the ballroom. 'I realise the clock is about to strike midnight, so I won't keep you long.'

A ripple of laughter greeted this remark.

'I'm taking this opportunity to introduce you to the woman I intend to marry.'

Not the woman he loved, Callie thought, cursing herself for being such a doubter. Luca had to wait a moment until the exclamations of surprise had died down.

'Signorina Callista Smith is an exceptional woman, whom I am lucky to have found.'

As he beckoned Callie forward and she joined him in the centre of the ballroom, the surprise of the sophisticated onlookers gradually turned to muted applause. They were shocked to the heels of their highly polished footwear, she thought as

Luca lifted his hands for a silence that had already fallen deep and long.

'It goes without saying,' he added, 'that all of you will receive an invitation to our wedding.' He gave a fierce, encouraging smile into Callie's eyes, before turning back to address his riveted audience. 'I invite you all to enjoy the rest of your evening, while I continue to celebrate with my beautiful fiancée.'

As if by magic the orchestra struck up a romantic Viennese waltz, which allowed Luca to prove that not only could he sweep Callie off her feet, but he could provide the prompt necessary to shake everyone out of their stupefied trance, and soon the dance floor was ablaze with colour and the flash of precious jewels.

Callie told herself that everything would work out. Yes, there would be problems, but they'd get through them. Luca was right. This was the best solution. It was only when the clock struck midnight, and he was briefly distracted by one of the many ambassadors present, that everything changed.

She'd seen pictures of Max in various magazines back home. In the flesh, he was even more striking. As tall as Luca, he looked quite different, which was only to be expected when they weren't related by blood. Where Luca's features were rugged and sexy, Max's face was thin and hard, and, quite unlike Luca, Max's manner was unpleasantly autocratic.

Dressed entirely in black, his blood-red sash of office the only bright thing about him, Max was the haughtiest man in the room by far. And he was heading her way surrounded by cronies, all of whom were viewing Callie with what she could only describe as amused contempt. There was a beautiful woman on Max's arm, who was also dressed in black, with the addition of half a hundredweight of diamonds. Her tiara alone could have settled most countries' debts, Callie guessed. Knowing she was the target of the advancing party, she stood her ground and lifted her chin, then shrank inwardly when Max stopped directly in front of her.

'Well, my dear,' he said, keeping his stare fixed on Callie as he turned to address his obviously heavily pregnant companion, 'this is the little snip my brother intends to put on our throne.'

'Surely not?' his elegantly dressed companion protested as she stared disapprovingly at Callie. 'Who is she, anyway? And *where* did she get that dress?'

Callie ground her jaw, refusing to demean herself by responding. Max's friends could laugh all they liked. They wouldn't drive her away.

'Goodness knows, my dear,' Max replied, still staring at Callie through mocking eyes. 'Perhaps she got it from the same thrift store that sold her the dye for that ridiculous hair colour.'

As everyone laughed Callie reached up instinctively to touch her hair, and regretted the lapse immediately. She hated letting them see they'd upset her. 'Well, at least I don't have a cruel tongue,' she said mildly.

'Oh, she speaks,' Max exclaimed, turning to look at his friends. 'I imagine she learned that skill in *the pub back home*.' He made each vowel sound grotesque and ugly.

As Max and his friends roared with laughter, Callie made sure to remain impassive.

'He only keeps her around because she's pregnant,' Max drawled, quirking a brow in an attempt, Callie thought, to elicit some sort of response from her. 'He's desperate for an heir, and when you're as desperate as Luca I suppose it's a case of any port in a storm. Seeing you pregnant,' he added to the woman at his side, 'must really have disturbed him. That's the only reason he's chosen this girl. He's trying to compete with me—imagine that?'

'He's quite obviously failed,' one of Max's cronies derided.

'That's all this is,' Max assured Callie, bringing his cruel face close. 'Don't think for one moment that you've bagged yourself a prince, let alone that this is a fairy tale. This is a cold-blooded transaction, my dear. Luca doesn't want you. He doesn't want anyone. The only thing Luca wants is an heir. That's the only way he can hope to keep the throne of Fabrizio. It's written into our constitution. Two years, one baby at least, or I take over.' Coming even closer, he sneered. 'You're nothing more than a convenient womb. Shall we?' he added to his gloating companions with an airy gesture. 'I've had enough of this ball. The quality of guests at the palace has really gone down. The casino beckons. A few spins of the wheel holds far more appeal than these provincials can ever hope to provide me.'

'She's gone? What do you mean, she's gone?' Luca stared down at Michel in surprise. The elderly retainer seemed more than usually confused. 'Take your time, Michel. I'm sorry. I didn't mean to shout at you.'

'I saw her talking to Max,' Michel told him in a worried tone.

'What?'

'You said you wouldn't shout,' Michel reminded him.

'You're right,' he admitted, placing a reassuring hand on the older man's shoulder. 'But who invited Max?'

'Does Max need an invitation to visit his family home?'

Luca ground his jaw. He should have known that Max would never keep to their agreement that he stay out of Fabrizio. 'So, where the hell is she?' he repeated as he raked his hair with tense fingers.

'I saw her running out of that door not ten minutes ago,' Michel informed him, staring across the ballroom towards the French doors leading onto the garden and then the lake. 'And that was straight after talking to Max.'

'Ten minutes?' Luca exclaimed, frowning. 'Did I leave her alone for that long?'

'The ambassador can be garrulous and difficult to get away from,' Michel said in an obvious attempt to placate him. 'And His Excellency was more than usually talkative tonight.'

Luca could not be placated. His one concern was Callie. He should have told her long before now what she meant to him. The convenient plan that had fallen into place when he found out she was pregnant hadn't figured in his thinking when he'd made the announcement that they would be married.

All right, so maybe it had, he conceded grimly as he made a visual search of the ballroom to make sure she'd gone. Would he stick around under similar circumstances? So, where could she be? In her room, or had she tried to return to the island? His heart banged in his chest at the thought that she might have taken the rowing boat. Navigation was easy for him in the dark. He'd been rowing on the lake for most of his life. So he knew about the clinging weeds and treacherous rocks. If Callie took the wrong route, she could be in serious trouble. He didn't wait to consider his options. Cutting through the crowd, he hurried away.

He ran to the shore. The boat was gone. There was no sign of Callie. Everyone had been shocked by his announcement of their engagement, and now Max was causing trouble again. He had a stark choice to make. Callie, or the future of Fabrizio. There was no choice. Stripping off his clothes, he dived into the lake.

Relief surged through him when he spotted her pacing the shore. 'Callie,' he exclaimed, springing out of the water. Striding up to her, he seized hold of her and demanded she look at him. 'What's wrong? What happened back there?'

'You happened,' she said.

Her voice was faint, but the fire in her eyes was

brighter than ever. She was hurt, bitterly hurt. He knew all the signs. Max had always been an expert when it came to wounding with words.

'Thank you for telling me how badly you needed an heir,' she said tensely, sarcastically.

'Meaning?' he demanded.

'I'm told your constitution demands it, if you're to keep the throne.' There were tears of anger and distress in her eyes. 'I would have been quicker off the mark getting pregnant, if you'd told me.'

'Don't be ridiculous,' he flared. 'What on earth has Max said to you?'

'Only the truth, I believe.'

A muscle jerked in his jaw. He couldn't even deny it, and had to listen to his brother's poison flooding from Callie's mouth.

'Max said that making an heir is the only reason you had sex with me.'

'I didn't have sex with you,' he insisted. 'I made love to you.'

'Maybe.' She hesitated a little. 'But how do I know that's true, now I know you had a motive?'

'Why can't you believe in yourself, Callie? Why won't you believe how much I need you?'

'Because it's convenient for you to have me,' she exclaimed. 'A convenient womb, Max called me. He says your primary concern is to build a dynasty.'

'My primary concern is you,' he argued fiercely.

'It doesn't feel that way to me, Luca. You made the announcement of our engagement without asking me first, without giving me chance to consider what I'm getting into. My late father used to tell me what I could and couldn't do, and I swore that I would never fall into that trap again.'

'This isn't a trap. You're not thinking straight, Callie.'

'I'm thinking perfectly,' she fired back. 'It's just a pity I haven't been thinking perfectly from the start.'

'That's your hormones talking.'

'Don't you dare,' she warned him. 'What was your plan, Luca? We marry, I have the baby, and then your people organise a convenient divorce? You don't have much time to play with, do you? Pregnancy sets a clock ticking, and so does the constitution of Fabrizio, Max tells me. Tonight was the perfect opportunity for you to announce our engagement. I imagine you'd have had us married by the end of the month, so that everything would be finalised before my pregnancy becomes obvious.'

He couldn't argue. So much of what she said was true, but his feelings when he'd discovered Callie was pregnant had been real and strong. A baby. A child. A family. Everything he'd always dreamed of had been suddenly within his reach. For a man used to subduing or ignoring his emotions, he'd been overwhelmed, and not just because Callie would provide him with the longed-for heir. She was the perfect woman, who would become the perfect mother. She would be his perfect bride, and would transition seamlessly into a much-loved princess. 'What's so terrible about becoming my wife?'

'If you don't know,' she said, sounding sad, 'I can't tell you. I suggest you forget about me, and ask one of those princesses to be your wife. You'll hardly be short of replacements for me.'

'Aggravating woman!' he roared. 'I don't want a replacement. I want you.'

'You can't have everything you want, Luca.'

'Are you saying no?' he demanded with incredulity.

'I'm saying no,' Callie confirmed.

'But you'll be a princess.'

'Of what?' she demanded. 'All you're offering is a temporary position, an empty life in a foreign country with a man who only wants me for my child-bearing capabilities.'

'That's Max talking. Don't listen to him.'

'I don't want that for our child,' she said, ignoring him, 'and I don't want to be a princess in a loveless marriage. I can't snuggle up to a tiara at night. I'd rather be back home in one room with my baby.'

'That isn't your choice to make,' he said, adopting a very different tone.

'Are you threatening me?' she said quietly.

'I'm reminding you that you're carrying the heir to the principality of Fabrizio, and that neither you nor I can change that fact.'

'And thank God for it,' she whispered as blood drained from her face. 'But there is something I can do.'

'Which is?' he demanded suspiciously.

'Unless you intend to keep me here by force, I can return home to spend Christmas with friends I can trust. You took my trust and abused it,' she accused. 'And tonight I learned that you took my body and used that too.'

'*What? Dio!* Never!' He raked his still-damp hair with frustration. 'Don't we know each other better than this? Yes, passion drove us initially. And yes, your pregnancy was convenient. I won't deny it. But it means so much more to me now. *You* mean so much more. I'm still coming to terms with the fact that I feel—' He stopped. He couldn't even put into words how many feelings he was dealing with. For a man who'd spent most of his life avoiding emotion, he was drowning in them. 'I respect you and I always will,' he stated firmly. 'Please give some thought to what becoming my wife will mean.'

'I have,' Callie assured him quietly, 'and it's not what I want.'

'What do you want?' he demanded fiercely. He'd do anything to put this right.

'I want love and respect on both sides,' she said without hesitation. 'I want friendship that makes both of us smile, and I want trust like a rock we can both depend on. I want to honour the man who is my lover, my friend, and the father of my child, as he honours me. And I want my independence. I've fought too hard to lose that now.'

'You'll have it as my wife,' he asserted confidently.

'And as your Princess?' When he didn't answer, because he knew only too well the restrictions that royal life imposed, she continued, 'I've spent too much of my life caged, and I won't exchange one cage for another, however big an upgrade that might seem to you. And it's not what I want for our child. I want us all to be free. I know I'm a fantasist,' she added in a calmer voice, 'and I know I want too much. I should have realised that from the start.'

'Callie!'

'No. Don't try to stop me,' she called back as she ran back to the lake. 'We were never meant to be together. Max is right. I can't marry a prince—this is over,' she flared, trying to shake him off when he caught up with her.

'It doesn't need to end here,' he said firmly, holding her still.

'Yes, it does.' With a violent tug she broke free. 'Goodbye, Luca—'

'But I love you.'

She stopped on the edge of the lake. Whether she intended to swim back or row back, he had no idea. He did know she was furious. 'You love me?' she said tensely. 'Yet you didn't think to tell me this before tonight? It sounds like you're desperate to keep me here.'

'I am desperate, but not for the reasons you think. You're more to me than you could ever know, more than Max could even comprehend.'

She shook her head. 'You had to be sure of me, didn't you, Luca? That's why you made the announcement of our engagement tonight in front of so many witnesses.'

'You're not listening, Callie. I love you. And you're right. I should have told you long before now, but I didn't realise it myself. I didn't recognise the symptoms,' he admitted ruefully, raking his hair with frustration. 'I'm not exactly familiar with love in all its guises.'

'Your father didn't love you?' she challenged with an angry gesture.

'The Prince loved me, but it wasn't easy for me to trust him enough to return his love, not as soon as he wanted, anyway.'

'He must have been a patient man.'

'He was.'

'Know this, Luca. Nothing will change my mind. I don't want a work in progress, while you discover your feelings. I want the boy who made his home in the Coliseum and dreamed of what he would one day become. I want the man who made that happen. Don't you dare make your past an excuse. I haven't.'

That was true. She shamed him. 'How can I prove that I love you?'

'By letting me go,' she said with her usual frankness.

Back home at the Browns', the ache in Callie's heart at the absence of Luca was like a big, gaping wound that refused to heal. Even the Browns' famously over-the-top Christmas preparations couldn't do anything to mend it. Seeing Anita again had helped, Callie conceded as she smiled across the room at her friend from the lemon groves. Anita had become a most welcome fixture at the Browns'. On her return, Callie had persuaded Anita, who lived alone in a rented room, to take a job close by, and the Browns had offered to rent her a room. They always welcomed help with the younger children and Anita would never be alone again, Ma Brown had promised. Anita had a proper family now—if she could stand the noise and chaos. Anita could certainly do that, and had fitted right in.

'Come on, our Callie,' Ma Brown insisted as she bustled into the room they called the front parlour. 'Anita, I need you to help me in the kitchen, and, Rosie, you and Callie still have the rest of those crêpe paper streamers to hang.'

'And make,' Rosie pointed out as she glanced at the uncut reams of crinkled paper and then at Callie's preoccupied face. 'Come on, I'll help you.' Kneeling down at Callie's side, Rosie waited until her mother had left the room before putting an arm around Callie's shoulders. 'I know you haven't said anything in front of the family, but you can't keep bottling this up. And you can't keep refusing to speak to him,' Rosie added. 'If Prince Luca comes to England to see you—'

'Do you know something?' Callie asked. Her heart soared at the thought of seeing Luca again, even as her rational mind told her she could never be a princess, so it was better not to see him at all.

'Not exactly,' Rosie admitted uncomfortably. 'I'm just saying that if Luca did turn up, you should see him.'

'I don't have to see anyone,' Callie argued stubbornly, but her heart was beating so fast just at the thought of seeing Luca again that she could hardly breathe. Was he in the country, maybe somewhere close by? There was no smoke without fire, she concluded, glancing at Rosie, who refused to meet her eyes.

'We'd better get these streamers made,' Rosie said, acting as if the lack of paper decorations was the only crisis looming, 'or there'll be hell to pay.'

CHAPTER TWELVE

CALLIE FROZE. THEY had just sat down to the most mouth-watering Christmas feast when an imperative knock sounded at the door.

'I'll answer it,' Pa Brown insisted when Callie moved to get out of her chair.

'Let him go,' Ma Brown said to everyone with a calming gesture. 'Whoever's there, we can't leave a stranger on the doorstep today.'

That was no stranger, Callie thought, shivering inwardly with excitement as the distinctive sound of Luca's dark, husky voice made everyone sit up and take notice. The air changed, stilled, and was suddenly charged with electricity as, quite improbably, His Serene Highness, Prince Luca of Fabrizio, stood framed in the narrow doorway. Radiating glamour, presence, and an irrational amount of heat, Luca was a starry visitor to the homey Christmas at the Browns'. His stare locked briefly with Callie's. That short look carried more heat, more passion and determination than she could stand. It was almost a relief when he turned to greet everyone else in the room.

'This is wonderful,' Luca exclaimed, sucking in a deep, appreciative breath as Pa Brown relieved him of his rugged jacket. 'I didn't realise how hungry I was, until I smelled this delicious food.' His gaze swept over Callie before he smiled at Ma Brown. 'Do you have room for one more?'

'Most certainly,' Ma Brown exclaimed, leaping up from the table.

In a midnight-blue fine-knit sweater that clung lovingly to his magnificent frame, and beat-up jeans moulding his muscular thighs, Luca was an improbable giant in their midst. Callie couldn't help but remember having those thighs locked around her as they made love, and her longing for Luca surged as his stare found hers and this time lingered. Her heart was gunned into action. She hadn't realised how much she'd missed him. Snow dusted his ink-black hair, making it twinkle and gleam. If she'd never met him before and didn't know his history, if someone had told her that Luca was a cage fighter she'd have believed them. He certainly wasn't her childhood idea of Prince Charming. But fairy tales were a long way behind them now. Sex radiated from him like sparks from a Catherine wheel, though his eyes were full of warmth for the Browns, and for Anita. 'Don't I know you from Italy?' he asked Anita.

'You do, Your Serene Highness,' Anita admitted, blushing.

'Call me Luca,' he said. 'You know the rules.'

As Anita and Luca laughed together, Callie thought him so infectiously warm, so vital and compelling. 'I hope I'm not intruding,' he said, noticing that the Browns were all staring at him open-mouthed.

'Not at all,' Pa Brown was quick to reassure him.

'Good,' Luca declared, 'because I'm here to claim my bride.'

The younger Browns stared at Luca, while the rest carried on as if nothing unusual had occurred. Callie moved first. Pushing her chair back, she put down her napkin. If it hadn't been for Pa Brown's restraining hand on her shoulder, she would have left the room and taken Luca with her. What right did he have to come storming in like some medieval feudal lord, interrupting the flow of everything around the Christmas table and demanding that she be his bride. 'Steady girl,' Pa Brown murmured discreetly.

Everyone closed their mouths and pretended to concentrate on their food as Callie sat down again. All except one. 'You can have my chair, if I can have a ride in your sports car,' young Tom Brown told Luca.

'Sounds like a deal to me,' Luca agreed with a smile.

'My name's Tom,' the youngster supplied as he and Luca bumped fists.

'Come on, everyone…shuffle up,' Ma Brown instructed. 'Let's make room for the Prince.'

'Now, there's a phrase you don't hear said every day,' Pa Brown ventured, only to receive a stern look from his wife.

For a while everything was good-natured chaos as chairs were swopped around, and new cutlery was brought out of the drawer. Once crockery and glassware had been located, everything was settled for their guest.

'I envy you,' Luca told his hosts midway through the most succulent meal of turkey with all the trimmings.

'You envy us?' Pa Brown exclaimed, only to receive a second hard stare from his wife, who sensibly steered the situation.

'More gravy with that extra helping of meat, Luca?'

'Yes, please.'

With Ma Brown setting the tone, all the Browns began to behave as if His Serene Highness were any other neighbour who'd called around to share their Christmas cheer. Now that was class, Callie thought. Stuff Max and his cronies. They couldn't hold a candle to these genuine folk. The meal could have been tense, and Christmas could have been ruined, but with Luca at his relaxed best, and Anita and the Browns just being themselves, the irreverent, good-natured banter soon resumed.

'So, what's it like being a prince?' young Tom enquired.

'Busy,' Luca told him economically.

'Don't you have to smile at people you don't like?' another boy asked.

'That's called diplomacy,' Pa Brown put in. 'Something you could all do with a lesson in.'

'No, he's right,' Luca intervened. 'That's why it's so good to be here.' He flashed a wry glance at Callie, who raised a brow.

'Didn't you have anywhere else to go at Christmas but here?' young Tom demanded.

Luca's lips quirked as he thought about this. 'I had a few places, but nowhere as special as here.'

'Pudding?' Ma Brown enquired.

'Yes, please,' Luca confirmed. 'But first...' He glanced at Callie, and then jerked his head towards the door.

'Of course,' Ma Brown agreed. 'I'll keep the pudding warm for both of you.'

Callie wasn't sure how she felt. She didn't feel any more forgiving towards Luca, but they did need to talk, and the sooner, the better.

'So now you know,' she said. Having wrapped

herself up warmly in her winter coat and scarf, she was sitting in the front seat of Luca's bright red car.

'Know what?' he asked with a frown as he started the engine.

'Where I come from.'

'You're lucky. It's wonderful. That's the best Christmas I've ever been part of.'

'And it hasn't even started yet,' Callie said wryly. 'Wait until they start playing parlour games.'

'Parlour games?' Luca queried.

'What people used to do before TV.'

He shot her a sideways look. 'Sounds interesting.'

'You said you'd give me time, Luca,' she reminded him as he pulled into the light Christmas Day traffic.

'How much time do you need?'

'More,' she insisted.

'I'm afraid that's not possible. I have other places to be.'

'You said you'd let me go.'

'I didn't say I wouldn't come after you.'

Callie shook her head while her heart went crazy. 'I belong here, Luca.'

'You belonged in the lemon groves too. You belonged in the five-star hotel, whether you chose to believe it or not. The staff there love you. You belong anywhere you choose to be. You have a positive slant on life that infects the people around you. That's why they love you. That's why I love you, and want you for my wife.'

'And a royal princess, mother of your heir,' she said quietly.

'So you're going to believe Max, not me.'

'I make my own decisions. This has nothing to do with Max.'

'Who has been reminded that he'd agreed to stay away from Fabrizio for life,' Luca explained, 'in case you were wondering.'

'Stop here.'

'What?'

'Here,' she insisted. 'There's a park. We can walk.'

Luca dipped his head to stare around. 'I had intended taking you somewhere more romantic.'

'It's all a matter of scale,' Callie insisted, 'and

this is fine. This patch of green might not look much to you, but I can tell you that it's appreciated around here as much as you appreciate your royal parks.'

'I didn't play in royal parks as a boy,' Luca reminded her as he slowed the car. Parking up, he killed the engine. Getting out, he came around to open the passenger door. She accepted his help and climbed out.

The same thrill raced up her arm. Luca's quiet strength was so compelling. He broke the silence first as they went through the entrance into the small inner-city park, and her breath caught in her throat when he said, 'I refuse to believe you don't know how right this is between us.'

'But you're a prince,' she protested.

'I'm a man.' Wrapping his big hands around her lapels, he drew her close. 'And that man knows we belong together. But though I've confided in you, you've told me nothing.'

Shoulders hunched against the freezing wind, Callie lifted her head and stared into Luca's strong, rugged face. 'Why do you want to marry me, when you can have your pick of every princess in the world, and all the heiresses, if that grand ball was anything to go by?'

'I keep asking myself that same question,' Luca admitted dryly.

'This isn't funny,' she said.

'This I know,' he agreed. 'All I can come up with is that there is no reason to love. You either do or you don't.'

They had stopped in front of the bandstand where, only that morning, she'd sung carols with the Browns while the local band played their hearts out.

'I know why you don't trust easily, Callie. You had a hard life with your father. Ma Brown told me a lot of it over the phone.'

'She shouldn't have.'

'Yes, she should,' he argued. 'She cares about you, and the Browns thought I should know. When you didn't answer my letters, I got in touch with them. They told me to stay away and give you time to take everything in. Has it worked?' He gave her a fleeting smile.

'And love,' she said. 'What conclusion did you come to?'

He considered her question. 'I came to the conclusion that love isn't rational, and there are no answers. There's only this…' Dragging her close, he kissed her, gently to begin with, and then with increasing fire, until they were kissing each other as if they were the last two people on earth.

It felt as if they were finding each other all over again. 'I've missed you,' she breathed when they finally broke apart.

'You have no idea,' Luca murmured as he smoothed her hair back from her face. 'When I say that I want to know all about you, I'm not talking about the heavily edited facts you've fed me in the past, but the truth, all of it, good and bad. I want to face the trials and triumphs together, so we can share the feelings we've both steered clear of in the past. I'm still learning when it comes to emotion, but I owe it to my country to change, and I owe it to you most of all. If we don't know sadness, how can we recognise happiness, and if we don't feel regret, how can we look forward and plan for the future? Tell me everything,' he insisted. 'I'll know if you're holding back.'

She thought back, and started with her mother. 'I can't remember her...' She paused, saddened. 'My father blamed me for her loss. She died in childbirth,' Callie explained. 'And he could have been so much more,' she said as she thought about her father.

'But none of this is your fault,' Luca insisted. Taking hold of her hands, he brought them to his lips and kissed them. 'You don't need to tell me how hard you've worked. Your hands speak for you.'

Callie laughed ruefully. She didn't exactly have a princess's hands. They were red and work-worn, having never quite recovered from scrubbing floors at the pub, but they were part of her, and she would rather have her work-roughened hands than all the pale, floaty things she'd seen at the ball.

'What was life like before your father died?' Luca prompted when she fell silent.

'Life's always been great, thanks to the Browns. Well, most of it,' she conceded. 'But if I didn't have the Browns...' That didn't bear thinking about.

'Good friends are beyond price,' Luca agreed. 'But now you have to ask yourself what *you* want out of life now.'

You, she thought, but you without complications, and she knew that wasn't possible. 'I wish life were simpler,' she said. 'I wish we could go back to working in the lemon groves, when I thought we were both holiday staff.'

'We're the same people we were then.'

'But now you're a prince,' Callie argued.

'I'm a man in love with you.'

Or in love with the thought of great sex going forward with the woman carrying his child? she wondered. 'I just don't know if it could work out,' she said, speaking her doubts out loud. 'The Princess bit, I mean.' Lifting her chin, she stared directly at Luca. 'Being royal seems so confining to me.'

'Not once you learn how to pin on a tiara,' he said. 'I'm sure you'll soon get the hang of it.'

She shot him a warning look, but Luca was in no way deterred. 'I've got homes across the world where we can be alone as much as you want, and I've got a superyacht to escape to.'

'That's just the point, isn't it? This is all normal to you, but it's crazy mad to me.'

'So?' he prompted.

'So, no, thank you.'

'Think about it carefully.'

'I have,' she assured him.

'I realise it's a huge commitment to make. Most people would jump at the chance of marrying into royalty and wouldn't give a second thought to the practicalities. But that's not you, Callie. You're cranky, challenging, and real, and that's why I want you at my side.'

'Compliments?' she said dryly. It was hard to remain neutral when Luca was working his charm. She was already warming and thrilling inside, and she didn't need anyone to tell her how dangerous that was. 'Or are you saying I keep your feet on the ground?'

'That's not the reason I want you,' Luca assured her with one of his dark, gripping looks. 'And, in the interest of clarity, I should make it clear that your feet won't be on the ground for long.'

* * *

'So,' Callie murmured, shooting him a troubled look when they got back in the car. 'You love me.'

'I do.'

'And you want to marry me.'

'Correct.'

'And not just because I'm pregnant with your convenient heir?'

Pressing back in the driver's seat, Luca sighed heavily. He owed her nothing less than the truth. 'When I first found out, I'll admit that it suited my plan.'

'You needed an heir,' she supplied.

'Yes, I did. And great sex.'

'Luca—'

'Regularly.'

'You're impossible.'

'Seriously?' he asked. 'If you want to know what I want? I want a family like the Browns.'

'Fourteen children?'

'One at a time?' he queried, sliding her a look. 'That's not so bad.'

'For you, maybe,' Callie said, biting back a

smile. But then she turned serious. 'Callie from the docks, the Princess of Fabrizio?'

'Callie from the lemon groves, and my beloved wife,' Luca argued as he pulled away from the kerb. 'So, what's your answer, Callie?'

'The same as it was before,' she said tensely. 'I still need time to think.'

'All you need is time to assess your character and abilities to realise that you have everything it takes and more to be my Princess. So I'll give you until we get to the Browns', and then I want your answer.'

'And if it's no?' she pressed.

'We'll deal through lawyers in the future.'

Her face paled. 'That sounds like a threat.'

'It's the only practical option I can come up with. Or you can give me your answer now, if you prefer?'

She refused to be drawn, and by the time he had stopped the car outside the Browns', he could feel Callie's tension. Helping her out of the low-slung vehicle, he kept hold of her hand as they walked to the front door. Each time they talked, he learned a little bit more about her, and what he'd learned today had confirmed his opinion that they weren't so different. They both had principles, loyalty, and trust printed through them like sticks of rock. Callie was honest to a fault, and still overcoming the scars of a difficult childhood. He'd had the most enormous stroke of luck when he'd met the Prince at the Coliseum, and Callie had experienced a small taste of luck with her surprise win on the scratch card that had allowed her to travel to the lemon groves. It was strange how fate set things in motion. Experience had taught him that sometimes it paid to go with the flow.

'Come in, come in,' Pa Brown invited as he threw the front door wide.

Luca might live in a palace with servants on every side, but he hadn't been joking when he said that he envied the Browns. This was the type of family he had imagined being part of when he was a boy on his own each night with only the ghosts from the past for company. He and Callie were welcomed back into the warm heart of the Brown family just as the Christmas gifts were being opened and happy noise was at its height.

Dogs and children were racing around colliding with each other, while Anita tried in vain to keep up with the amount of wrapping paper flying through the air. Rosie was attempting, without much success, to dissuade the younger Browns from opening each of the crackers before they were pulled, to discover what gifts lay inside.

'We saved some crackers for you,' she explained to Callie and him, as Pa Brown insisted on taking Luca's jacket.

'And I've saved two big dishes of plum pudding,' Ma Brown added from the doorway.

'I'd like a few moments of Ma and Pa's time. If I may,' he said.

Silence dropped like a stone. Every head turned his way, and then the focus switched to Callie, who shrugged, giving him no clue as to what her answer would be to his proposal.

'Of course,' Pa Brown agreed, breaking the tension as he exchanged a look with his wife. 'Come into the kitchen where we can be private, Luca. Would you like Callie to join us?'

'No. It's something I want to ask both of you. It involves Callie, but she knows all about it.'

'Do I?' Callie demanded, making him wonder yet again if he had misjudged the moment.

She was unreadable, and where women of his acquaintance were concerned that was a novelty, and, for a man who had everything money could buy, novelty was the most valuable currency of all.

'You should know how I feel about you by now,' he insisted, and, grabbing her close, he kissed her, which in front of the younger Browns was tantamount to making a public announcement.

Before he had chance to leave for the kitchen, young Tom piped up, 'You'll need this…' Holding out a blue plastic ring from his cracker, Tom stared up at Luca expectantly.

'*Grazie!* Thank you, Tom. Your timing couldn't be better.' He stowed the ring away in the back pocket of his jeans, and left Callie to have his conference with the Browns. When he came back, he knelt at Callie's feet—which wasn't as easy as it sounded with all the toys scattered around. 'Will you do me the very great honour of accepting this priceless ring, which has been especially chosen for you by Signor Tom?'

'I'm overwhelmed,' Callie admitted, starting to laugh.

The situation was bizarre admittedly, and could only happen, he figured, at Christmas. 'Take it,' he muttered discreetly, 'or I won't be responsible for my actions.' As the younger Browns cheered he sprang up and put the ring on Callie's finger. There were a few tense moments when she didn't say a word, but then she laughed and threw her arms around his neck, and everyone cheered.

'A Christmas wedding, then,' Ma Brown exclaimed, clapping her hands with excitement.

'A bit late for Christmas, Ma. It will have to be New Year,' Pa Brown, who should have known he could never win, argued, frowning.

'Ah, that's where you're wrong,' Ma Brown assured him, 'because Christmas is celebrated in January in Fabrizio. Isn't that right, Luca?'

'Quite correct, Mrs Brown.'

'Still, not much time,' Ma Brown said, frowning as she thought about it. 'But enough time, if I know our Callie.'

'You do know Callie,' Luca asserted, giving

Ma Brown the warmest of hugs. 'You know her better than anyone except me.'

'I'll accept that,' Ma Brown stated as Callie narrowed her eyes in mock disapproval.

'How long have you three been conniving?' Callie enquired, raising a brow as she looked at Luca and then Ma and Pa Brown in turn.

'Four,' Rosie put in. 'Don't forget me.'

'Why, you—' Callie was still laughing when Luca swept her off her feet. Swinging her around, which was quite a risky manoeuvre in a room full of Browns and Anita, he planted a breath-stealing kiss on her mouth. 'Have you kept my letters?' he asked as he set her down. 'I was just thinking that you might want to read them now.'

'Read them *now*?' Rosie exclaimed. 'The paper they're written on is almost worn through. Don't let Callie kid you, Luca. You are the love of Callie's life.'

EPILOGUE

IT WAS UNSEASONABLY cold in the north of England. Brilliant white snow was falling in soft, silent drifts, slowing the traffic and muffling the noise of hooves as Callie's horse-drawn wedding coach arrived outside the Browns'. To counterbalance the frigid temperatures, every house on the street was brilliantly lit to celebrate the holiday season, which would go on well into the New Year. In the town, stores and corner shops were still crammed with reindeer and stars, and sleighs and plump-cheeked Santa Clauses, as if no one could bear to let go of the Christmas cheer.

There would never be another wedding like this one, Callie was sure of that. She was going to marry Luca in the area where she'd grown up, surrounded by her closest friends the Browns, Callie's landlady from the shop in Blackpool, and Anita, and Maria and Marco, who had travelled from Italy. She was wearing a dress chosen by Ma Brown and approved by Rosie. In ivory lace, it fitted her like a second skin—something she wouldn't be able to indulge in for very much longer, Callie thought, smoothing her hands over her slightly rounded stomach as Rosie arranged her veil.

The ceremony would be a simple affair in the local church, followed by a small reception at the Browns'. Callie had wanted the people closest to her to know how much they meant to her, and that even when she became a princess and lived in the palace in Fabrizio, they would still be a big part of her life. As far as the world of royalty was concerned, Callista Smith would marry Prince Luca of Fabrizio at a grand ceremony in that country's cathedral in a couple of weeks' time.

'You look beautiful,' Pa Brown said as he took charge of the young woman he thought of as a daughter. 'I'll be a proud man giving you away—though I'm only lending you out,' he added, frowning. 'I want you to keep in touch, our Callie, and never lose sight of your roots.'

'I never will,' she promised, giving Pa Brown a warm kiss on the cheek as Rosie draped a warm, faux-fur cape around Callie's shoulders. 'And you must all come and visit me regularly in Fabrizio.'

'Only if I can watch the match while I'm there,' Pa fretted with a frown.

'I'm sure it can be arranged,' Callie soothed, knowing how much the Saturday football match meant to Pa Brown.

They stepped out of the house straight into a snowdrift. Callie howled with laughter as she pulled her foot free from the glistening snow. 'Not a great start,' she admitted, 'but nothing can spoil today.'

The day was so Christmassy, with crisp snow underfoot and robins chirruping in the trees. It was so evocative of all the optimism inside her. Luca had insisted she must travel to the local church by horse and carriage and she was glad of the hot-water bottle waiting for her beneath the blankets on the leather seat. Two beautiful dapple-grey ponies with white plumes attached to their headbands were waiting patiently to draw her to the church. There were silver bells on their bridles that jingled as they trotted along. People stopped to stare, and waved frantically with friendly approval when they recognised the local girl who was soon to become a princess.

She'd never change, Callie thought. She'd always be Callie from the docks and Callie from the lemon groves too. All that mattered was love and friendship, and the man waiting for her inside the church.

Luca's face was full of pride when he turned around as the grand old organ struck up the wedding march. She had never seen anyone more handsome in her life. In a plain dark suit, without any of his orders of office, or the royal sash with its ornate jewelled insignia, Luca couldn't have looked hotter if he'd tried. What more could she want than this? Callie thought as Pa Brown transferred her hand from his to Luca's.

'You may kiss the bride.'

'I may kiss the love of my life,' Luca whispered so that only Callie could hear, 'the only Princess I'll ever need.'

'The only Princess you're ever going to get,' she teased him softly before they kissed. She stared down at the band of diamonds that Luca had whispered could never replace the blue plastic ring from the cracker, but he hope she liked it. Liked it? She loved it. And there will be another ring, he'd told her. 'When we marry in Fabrizio, you will have a ring made in Fabrizian gold.'

'The blue plastic ring was enough for me,' she had assured him. 'What I feel for you is in my heart.'

As they stepped outside the ancient church hand in hand, a crystalline scene of snow and icicles greeted them. Luca turned to Callie beneath the stone archway decorated with white winter roses and floating silk ribbons, to draw her winter bridal cape more snugly around her shoulders. 'Warm enough?' he asked.

She gave him one of her looks. 'Is that a serious question?'

Pulling her close against his muscular body, Luca gave Callie the only answer *she* would ever need, in a kiss that was more than hot enough to keep out any chill.

* * *

Michel, Luca's elderly aide, had advised on all things formal to make sure that protocol was followed for Luca and Callie's second ceremony in Fabrizio, but the magic, as always, was provided by the Browns, who had a far more relaxed take on what went into making the perfect wedding day. Callie only knew that it took one man to make her day perfect and he had just snuck into her suite at the palace, when she was fresh from the shower and naked beneath her fluffy towelling robe.

'You shouldn't be here,' she whispered, glancing over her shoulder to check that the door was securely locked.

'Why?' Luca demanded, looping his arms around her waist. 'You're not in your wedding dress, are you?'

'Exactly,' Callie exclaimed, shivering with desire as he teased the sensitive skin just below her ear with the lightest of rasps with his stubble. He looked beyond amazing, wearing nothing more than a white T-shirt and banged-up jeans. 'You parked the shave?' she reprimanded in between hectic gasps of breath.

'I know how much you like a good rasping,' he murmured, transferring his attention to her lips, which he now brushed with the lightest of kisses.

And she did like a good rasping. Far too much. 'You have to stop,' she gasped out.

'Or you won't be accountable for your actions?'

'Something like that,' she agreed on a dry throat as Luca's experienced hands traced the outline of her breasts.

'Do you know how long it is since we made love?' he demanded.

'Too long?'

'That's right,' he confirmed. 'It must be an hour since. What's this?' he asked, frowning as he extracted the fine gold chain that disappeared between her breasts.

'My something blue?'

'The plastic ring,' he exclaimed, smiling. 'I hope you won't mind if I replace it with something more substantial today?'

Callie's heart beat nineteen to the dozen. What type of rings did princesses have to wear? Her knowledge of such things was confined to magazines and newspapers, and those rings always looked so clunky and as if they would ruin all her clothes. 'So long as it's nothing too flashy.'

Luca hummed and frowned. 'I'm afraid I can't promise that.'

And Callie couldn't fail to be impressed. In fact, she was speechless when she saw the obviously priceless diamond ring that Luca had so casually pulled out from the back pocket of his jeans. The large, blue-white oval stone glittered wildly in the light as if it contained countless hopes and dreams just waiting to be set free. It was the most stunning piece of jewellery she'd ever seen, apart from the diamond ring Luca had surprised her with in the church in England. 'I don't need this,' she felt it only fair to tell him.

'But I want you to have it,' Luca insisted. 'Our children will expect you to have beautiful gifts from their father, a man who loves you more than anything else in the world.' As he spoke Luca placed his hand on her not quite so flat belly, as if he were making a pledge to both Callie and their baby to love and protect them with his life.

'You'll have to wear the engagement ring on your right hand with the eternity ring from England,' he said as he brought her fingers to his lips. 'According to tradition in Fabrizio, your wedding band goes on this left hand, because it is said to contain the vein the ancient Romans believed connected directly to your heart. We still call it the *vena amoris*, the vein of love, and for that finger you will wear something very different.'

'Fabrizian gold,' she said, remembering as their stares connected.

'As strong and as direct as you are,' Luca confirmed in a way that made her heart go crazy. Thrusting his hand for a second time into the back pocket of his jeans, he brought out the simple band. 'No frills,' he said. 'Just plain, honest perfection like you. I hope you enjoy wearing it.'

'I love it,' Callie exclaimed. 'You couldn't have chosen anything better. This is the most precious ring I'll ever wear.'

'And the plastic ring?'

'I'll never forget it, but this,' she said as Luca drew her close, 'will be the ring of my heart.'

He dipped his head to kiss her just as Ma

Brown called out from the other room, 'Are you ready to get dressed, Callie? We can't keep that carriage waiting.'

'Punctuality is the politeness of kings,' Luca teased.

'And my time-keeping's dreadful,' Callie fretted.

'Lucky for you I'd wait for ever if I had to.'

Luca had turned serious in a way that made her body ache for him, but with the briefest of kisses he was gone.

The second royal winter wedding was perfection, if a little grander than the first. The streets were packed with people eager to see their new Princess, and they weren't disappointed. There were food stalls and bands, and Christmas decorations still glittered everywhere. The theme was white and silver, which made everything seem filled with light. There might not be snow in Fabrizio at Christmastime, but beneath the flawless blue the gentle sunshine warmed the throngs of wedding guests as they cheered their new Princess dressed in yards of white silk chiffon that floated behind Callie as she walked along, and yet moulded her body so beautifully. The finest lace covered her arms and shoulders, while her train was almost twenty feet long. Anything shorter than that, and there wouldn't have been enough fabric for all the young Browns to take a handful of, Ma Brown had proclaimed ominously, but all the small bridesmaids and pageboys behaved perfectly on the day. There wasn't a spill or a smudge from any of them, and under the Browns' and Anita's prudent shepherding, Callie felt as if she were floating down the aisle of the glorious cathedral in Fabrizio before she finally halted at Luca's side.

'Who giveth this woman—'

'We do,' Pa Brown piped up, to be heartily shushed by his wife.

No one in the congregation noticed anything amiss, as they were all too busy watching the way Luca gazed at his bride. There was no doubt in anyone's mind that this was a royal love match, and one that would benefit all.

'Happy Christmas,' Luca murmured, and as Callie's gaze dropped instinctively to his mouth he added in a sexy whisper, 'Remind me. How long is it since we made love?'

'Too long,' Callie whispered back, her gaze locked on Luca's. 'Must be almost three hours now.'

'We may have to miss the reception,' he said with a mock frown.

'Almost certainly,' she agreed. And then the announcement rang out that His Serene Highness, Prince Luca of Fabrizio, could now kiss his bride.

'We may have to ask the congregation to leave,' Callie said dryly when Luca kissed her and she felt his very obvious impatience for herself.

Turning Callie, so that now they faced the packed body of the church together, Luca announced in a firm, strong voice, 'My Princess.' And as everyone applauded, he added, 'The love of my life.'

'There are no affairs of state for me to deal with for the next two weeks,' Luca told Callie as their horse-drawn carriage made its stately progress along the gracious main boulevard lined with cheering crowds. 'There's just my long-running affair with my wife to concentrate on now.'

'After our wedding feast,' she reminded him as she waved happily to the crowds.

'Did I mention we'll be delaying our arrival?'

'Really?' she asked, pretending to be shocked.

'I have commanded the carriage pause at our private entrance to the palace, so we have chance to…freshen up.'

'You think of everything,' Callie remarked dryly.

'I try to,' Luca confirmed.

If the staff at the palace was surprised by the sight of their Prince and Princess racing full tilt, hand in hand, across the grand hall, the bride with her tiara askew and her lengthy train bundled up beneath her arm, they of course made no comment. Minutes later, the happy couple had slammed their bedroom door behind them. Frantic seconds later Luca had opened every button down the back of Callie's beautiful gown. She barely had chance to remove her tiara before he swept her into his arms and carried her to the bed. The room was full of flowers and the scent was divine. 'And all for you,' he said.

'They're so beautiful,' Callie gasped when Luca gave her the briefest of chances to take everything in. 'Everyone's gone to so much trouble.'

'For you,' he declared as he took her deep, groaning with pleasure as she claimed him. 'For ever,' he whispered.

'Or even longer than that,' Callie agreed.

* * * * *

LET'S TALK
Romance

For exclusive extracts, competitions and special offers, find us online:

[f] facebook.com/millsandboon

[O] @millsandboonuk

[y] @millsandboon

Or get in touch on 0844 844 1351*

For all the latest titles coming soon, visit millsandboon.co.uk/nextmonth